Hawk and the Cougar

Tarah Scott

Chapter 1

Liz Williams slid into the last empty desk in the middle of the back row of the tiered lecture hall at Arizona State University. A low hum of conversation buzzed in the large room filled with university students nearly half her age. She hunched low in the seat. Dressed in jeans and a T-shirt, she blended in. *Almost.* She wanted to stay anonymous until the class finished. She'd taken the dress code cue from her daughter Emma who, despite being a genius, dressed like the teenager she was.

Emma had graduated high school three years ahead of schedule and gone directly to college. She'd started her undergrad education this semester. The kid was a machine, which was why Liz had been relieved to learn she had finally become interested in a young man. Until the conversation Liz had shamelessly eavesdropped on had taken a serious turn and she'd discovered the *young man* was Em's bioarcheology professor.

"Good in bed?" Emma had laughed into the phone. "Oh, yeah."

Liz's shock had been compounded when Emma told her

friend that Professor Hawkins would later join them at the dig where she was headed in Monument Valley.

For the thousandth time, Liz fretted that Emma had slipped out of thier home while Liz had been on a conference call with Leland Industries' Chicago clothing buyer. Darn the kid. Liz had tried reaching her without luck. Em was notorious for dropping her phone into her backpack and forgetting about it. Once she reached the mountains, there wouldn't be a signal for hours, if at all.

The door in the right-hand corner of the opposite wall opened, and the room quieted. Liz leaned to the right and peered down through the sea of bodies. She stilled at sight of the tall, broad-shouldered man entering the room. *This* couldn't be Professor Anthony Hawkins, PhD, the professor her daughter was having a relationship with. The picture on the university website had been taken on a dig. He'd stood in the distance, straw hat pulled low over his brow. His lean build had been obvious, but Liz had assumed the picture to be at least fifteen years old—maybe even older.

This man looked like he belonged in a time long past when Native American spirits roamed the desert. Jet black hair framed an angular face bronzed by countless hours of sun. The crisp white shirt and tight button-fly jeans he wore belied the sense of the ancient and emphasized the hard edge.

Light glinted off his belt buckle where a spider web, lime green, Apache cabochon stone was set inside a sterling silver cable design buckle. Before Liz realized the impulse, her gaze dropped to the generous bulge pressed against his fly. She flushed and yanked her gaze upward, where it snagged on a broad chest defined beneath his shirt.

He reached the desk and set the tan satchel he carried on top. He faced the blackboard, picked up a piece of chalk, and began writing. The shirt went taut across muscled shoulders.

His hair brushed the back of his collar, as if he'd waited just a little too long between haircuts. Liz's mouth went dry. She could almost feel the silky strands between her fingers as she fisted his hair with each thrust of his cock inside her.

The girl beside her released a low, but audible, "Ohhh."

Liz jarred from the erotic vision. She glanced around to see if anyone had caught her staring, but the students were intent on him. What had gotten into her? He had to be fourteen or fifteen years her junior—not the older man she'd assumed Emma was looking for to replace the father who walked out on them just after Em turned three.

This man was no father figure. Liz understood the attraction. What woman would be impervious to over six feet of tanned muscle? She couldn't deny his effect on her. But she was an adult and understood her reaction to be sheer lust. Just as he had to know better than to seduce his students.

As if sensing her stare, he faced the class and swung his gaze directly onto her. Liz slid lower behind her desk. He took a small step to the left and made eye contact again. What was she doing? She wasn't one of his young students to be intimidated. Despite the tremor that rippled through her, Liz kept her gaze locked with his and straightened. His brows rose in... amusement? Before she could be sure, his attention shifted to a student in the second row from the front.

"What are the four areas of investigation into cremated remains, as outlined by Charles Merbs?" he asked.

The student murmured an answer Liz couldn't hear over the thunder of her heart.

Fifty-five minutes later, Professor Hawkins ended the lecture, and everyone but Liz rose. She'd regained her composure. She would approach him reasonably. If he was stupid enough to risk his career over a seventeen-year-old kid, then he deserved everything she could dish out.

Five students waited to talk to him, four of whom were female. He answered their questions in a hushed tone, his eyes on the papers he stacked and put into his satchel. His gaze didn't so much as flick upward when the last young woman he spoke with leaned forward just enough to offer an inviting view of her impressive cleavage. He only asked if she needed anything else. The girl finally left, casting a murderous glance Liz's way as she passed her on the way to the door.

The door closed behind the girl, and he said, "If you're going to give Reid his money's worth, you'd better move your pretty ass. I have to be somewhere."

Liz froze. Reid? Money's worth? *Pretty ass?*

He picked up the satchel and headed for the door.

She jumped from her seat. "Hey!"

Liz hurried down the stairs. She reached the door as it clicked shut behind him and burst into the hallway. He was already halfway down the corridor. She sprinted after him with ease.

Thank you, Stairmaster.

He reached the exit a second before she did, and she slipped through the opening as the door nearly closed. Liz started forward, then hesitated. Two streetlights stood at each end of the deserted parking lot, but shadows hung heavy. Her heart raced. She couldn't let him go to Monument Valley without talking to him. She hurried forward and, seconds later, came up alongside him. His long strides forced her into a fast walk.

"We need to talk," she said.

He looked at her. "Talk? Come now, you don't get paid to *talk.*"

He stopped beside a beaten-up green Chevy truck, then

reached through the driver's side's open window, pulled up the handle, and opened the door.

"Listen, I came here hoping you'd see reason," she began.

He tossed his case inside and started to get into the truck. Liz couldn't believe it. He had no intention of giving her even five minutes. She seized the door, yanking it back so hard the old metal creaked. He stared for a long moment, then started to turn. Liz grabbed his arm. He shoved the door closed. Before she realized his intent, he had her against the car, arms stretched out on both sides so that she was trapped against the metal. Her pulse jumped into overdrive.

"You going to use that body to make me *see reason*?" His gaze raked down her length. "You'll get a lot further than Jack and his sidekick *The Beanstalk* did." He leaned so close his warm breath bathed her face. "Do you go all the way, sweetheart? Maybe even further? How much would that cost? My soul, maybe?"

"Cost—what the hell is wrong with you?" she demanded.

His brow lifted as it had in the lecture hall. "Well, well, you have a spine," he said, in a voice that told her it wasn't her spine he appreciated.

Liz straightened. He didn't move, and her breasts brushed his chest. Her nipples tightened. Surely, he couldn't feel her reaction through her lace bra and his shirt? Even if he did miss the rock-hard nipples that brushed his chest, he couldn't miss the hammering of her heart. A mental picture flashed of him towering over Emma as he was her and the kid melting in his arms.

Liz narrowed her eyes. "What university course does this fall under?" Surprise flicked across his face, and she couldn't resist a smug smile. "What's wrong? You don't know how to *educate* a real woman?"

"You want an education?" He leaned a hair's breadth

closer. Her nipples pressed into the steel of his chest. "I'd say so," he added in a low voice.

A warning bell went off in her head—too late. His arm shot around her, and he yanked her against him. His mouth crashed down on hers, hot, moist, *demanding*. Liz seized his shoulders and shoved, but he crushed her against the car, his belt buckle digging into her stomach. She shoved harder, and he jerked back.

She dragged in a breath, her flesh on fire where he'd gripped her arms. "You son of a bitch, I'll have you thrown in jail."

He barked a laugh. "Oh, that's rich. What will the charges read? 'Local professor arrested for dishing out the same treatment he got'?"

Liz poked at his chest. He backed up a step, as if she'd jabbed him with a shotgun. "It'll read 'attempted rape,' for starters." She jabbed again, and advanced when he retreated another step. "Then I'll pay a visit to," another jab, another step back, "Dean Manning."

He seized her wrist. "Listen, lady, I've had about all of this I'm going to take. You tell Reid—"

"All *you're* going to take?" She yanked free. The guy was insane. What kind of man had Emma gotten involved with? "You're finished."

He crossed his arms over his chest. "Is that a threat?"

Despite the quiver in her stomach, she gave him a disgusted look. "A promise."

He took the two steps to the driver's side door, reached inside, and pulled the lever. "Make all the promises you want but stay away from Manning. He's got nothing to do with this. He can't change my mind, and he's got no authority to override my decision. You tell Reid if he fucks with Manning, *or anyone*, he'll have the Native American Commission down on his head before he can say 'archaeological dig.'" He got into the truck.

Liz stared. "What are you talking about?" Something was very wrong. "I don't give a damn about the Native American Commission."

He turned on the engine. Headlights from a car entering the parking lot behind Liz cut across her body and illuminated his face. Professor Anthony Hawkins. *Anthony Hawkins.* The name had conjured pictures of a lanky intellectual who didn't have the slightest idea how to please a woman. This six feet of steel was anything but lanky, and his mouth alone would drive a woman wild. How much of Em's body had that mouth already explored?

"Stay away from Emma," Liz warned.

His brows snapped into a frown. "Emma?"

"Stay away from her."

"Emma Williams?"

Liz glanced over her shoulder at the approaching car. The black Suburban SUV made an unexpected swing in her direction. She jammed her eyes shut against the sudden intrusion of light.

"Move!" Professor Hawkins shouted.

Liz snapped her head around in time to see him leap from the truck. She whirled and faced the oncoming car. What felt like a brick wall crashed into her, and arms clamped around her like steel bands. They hit asphalt, her on top of him in unison with a deafening crash. Wheels screeched. Liz jerked her head up and gasped at the sight of the SUV backing up at full speed. The mammoth vehicle had rammed the Chevy!

The professor jumped to his feet, pulling her up with him, and lunged for the truck. She dug her heels in. He whirled, hauled her over his shoulder, and fairly leapt the few feet to the truck. He tossed her onto the seat as the SUV made a turn toward them.

"Move!" he shouted again, and she barely scooted over before he jumped in.

The Suburban came straight at them. He started the truck and jammed it into gear.

"What's going on?" Liz demanded.

"Hold on." He popped the clutch.

The Chevy shot backwards. Liz seized the dash to keep from flying forward, then braced herself when he hit the brakes and jammed into first gear. She dug a hand into the seat crevice in a frantic search for the seatbelt. Headlights filled the cab. She blinked against the glare of light as they raced forward, heading straight for the SUV.

She gripped the arm rest with her free hand, still braced on the dash with the other. "Have you lost your mind?"

He didn't flinch. Liz scanned for witnesses but saw no one else in the parking lot. She glanced at the professor. His eyes were straight ahead on the oncoming vehicle, body tense. He was going to do it. He was going to ram the SUV. She swung her gaze onto the speedometer. They were doing thirty-five. The SUV was fifty feet away. They would crash in seconds.

"For God's sake, pull off," she pleaded.

"They'll pull out."

Liz glanced at him. "You can't know that."

"Yes, I can."

Thirty feet.

Forty miles per hour. Liz looked out of the passenger side window. Asphalt sped past in a blur of black. She had a better chance of surviving the impact with the ground than a head-on collision in a vehicle that didn't have seatbelts, much less air bags.

Twenty feet.

She shoved open the door.

"What the hell—" he broke off.

Tires squealed, and the truck veered right. She slammed into Professor Hawkins. His arm shot around her, and he hugged her against him. Liz buried her face in his chest and clutched his shirt as they spun with the force of the empty truck bed. A hard jolt threw her forward, then yanked her back when he hit the brakes. He crushed her closer as they came to a jarring halt.

Liz remained motionless, eyes jammed shut, fingers gripping his shirt so tight her nails bit into her palm.

He twisted, his jaw brushing the top of her head as he looked over his shoulder. "Damn cowards," he muttered. "Hit and run." He relaxed back in the seat. "You all right?"

She inhaled a shaky breath, and her senses, filled with the aroma of fresh soap, mingled with an earthy scent that reminded her of the desert. Strong fingers cupped her chin and tilted her face upward. He stared down at her. Her heart hammered and her body trembled like an eight-point-nine earthquake. She fought the urge to bury her head in his chest again and burst into tears.

Liz dropped her gaze to his lips. His mouth lowered, then stopped a hair's breadth from hers. She lifted her eyes to his, and his brow rose. She straightened as if suddenly freed from a Jack-in-the-box. He jerked back, and she banged her head against the rear-view mirror. Dull pain radiated through her skull.

"Careful," he said. "You'll hurt yourself."

Liz rubbed the back of her head. "I'll hurt myself? You almost kill me, then tell me *I'll* hurt *myself?* What kind of nut are you? What the hell was that all about? I'm adding attempted murder to the charge of rape." She fingered the knot on her head.

He reached for the key. "Who are you?"

"The innocent act is getting old," she muttered.

He turned the key. The engine whined. He pumped the gas, and the motor kicked over. He shifted into gear and eased forward.

"Where are we going?" She glanced back at the building and the door they had exited.

"The door locks from the inside," he said. "You can't get back in that way."

"Just let me out here. I can walk to my car. I want to get as far away from you as possible."

"Soon enough." He made a slow turn out of the aisle. "What's this about me staying away from Emma Williams?"

She shot him a narrow-eyed look. "I know about the two of you."

"What do you know?"

"I know you have a relationship with her."

His attention remained straight ahead as he slowed for the exit. "I don't sleep with my students."

Liz gave a mirthless laugh. "I didn't expect you to tell the truth.'

"What's Emma to you?" he asked.

"She's my daughter."

He looked in her direction and raked his gaze down her in a quick but thorough appraisal. "Yeah, she's a wonder kid, only seventeen, but I wouldn't have pegged you for forty."

"I'm not," Liz snapped.

A corner of his mouth twitched. "No need to feel insulted. I said you looked younger."

She wasn't younger but was in no mood to explain—*didn't want to explain*—which only infuriated her more.

"You're a real sweet talker," she muttered.

He laughed, a deep, rich laugh that filled the small space.

"Cut me some slack. You caught me on a bad day." He stopped at the street and looked left, then right.

"You can let me out here," she said.

"Where's your car?" he asked.

Liz gave him a wary look.

"I'm not leaving you here," he said. "If those men come back, you don't want them making another run at you. They might not give up so easily."

A tremor flipped her stomach. "Who are they?"

He turned left onto the street and released a slow breath. "Did anyone ever tell you that you have lousy timing?"

She blinked. "What?"

He looked at her. "You picked the wrong day to play mother hen, sweetheart."

Chapter 2

The dark-haired beauty sitting beside Hawk did have lousy timing. They should be in a candlelit room, where they would dance well into the night before he took her back to his place to make love until dawn. But she'd picked tonight to accuse him of sleeping with her daughter. He preferred the mother. His cock pulsed with the erotic picture of the full-bodied brunette beneath him as he brought her to climax with sure, slow thrusts.

How badly had he screwed up his chances of getting her into that position? When he'd seen her in his class, he pegged her as Reid's second attempt to buy him with a high-priced call girl. The half a dozen young women who had been at the one and only meeting Hawk had agreed to with Reid couldn't have been more than twenty years old. Hawk had figured this woman was Reid's response to Hawk's comment that he didn't rob the cradle.

Hawk looked at her, careful to keep his eyes on her face and not the breasts that strained against the white T-shirt she wore. "Who told you I have a...relationship with your daughter?"

She hesitated.

"Can't be Emma," he said.

"Why not?"

He returned his attention to the road. "She strikes me as an honest kid."

She gave a deprecating laugh. "You're good."

"Emma didn't say we were having an affair. Did she?" he asked.

He glanced at her again and even in the dim streetlight, discerned the tinge of red coloring her cheeks. He'd seen too many young female students vie for his attention to believe Emma Williams had lied about their relationship. Despite the fact she was only an undergrad, Hawk had already assigned her senior projects. Had the mother read more into his actions than enthusiasm on his part to take a talented student under his wing and advise her through the PhD process?

Hawk slowed and downshifted as he turned left into the building's front parking lot. "When you get home, talk to your daughter. If there's any further misunderstanding, come see me."

"I'll be seeing you, all right, in the dean's office—then the police station," she snapped.

The dean's office would be for her daughter. The police station would be for nearly assaulting her. Yep, he'd screwed up.

"Where are you parked?" he asked.

"The north side of the lot. The blue Land Cruiser."

He pulled the truck around and slipped into park behind the older Toyota. She reached for the door.

"I thought Reid sent you," he said.

She looked at him. "Reid who?"

"Vance Reid," Hawk replied.

Recognition flickered across her face. "The land developer?"

He nodded. "Those were his boys who nearly ran you down."

She studied him. "What do they want?"

"They want me to say a dig outside Mesa is Navajo."

"Why should he care about one more Navajo site?" she asked. "There are loads of them. And what's that have to do with me?"

"Reid likes to sweeten the pot." Hawk shrugged. "I mistook you for one of the sweets."

She frowned, then her mouth dropped open. "Sweets? You think I'm a—" She clapped a hand over her mouth, and Hawk did a double take upon realizing she was stifling laughter.

"Most women would be insulted," he said.

The hand dropped away from her mouth. "I am." The obvious tightening of her lips against more laughter belied her words. "That's a terrible thing to say. I don't dress like a hooker."

"I didn't say hooker. High-priced call girl."

"There's no difference," she said.

"There's a huge difference."

She snorted. "Sure, and a multi-millionaire really is trying to kill you."

"That was four tons of steel coming at you," Hawk said, all humor gone. "I'd say they were trying to kill *you*."

Her eyes widened, and he should have regretted her fear but didn't. The last thing he wanted was her thinking he played chicken for fun. He leaned past her to the glove box. She jerked back into the corner as if he were a rattler. He paused and shifted his gaze to hers. She lifted her chin, and he resisted a smile. With some time, he'd find out what that fire felt like when he slid inside her. His body clenched at the thought of her walls tightening around him in climax. Damn it, he was two seconds away from making an even bigger fool of himself than he already had.

Hawk opened the glove box, pulled a card from those he'd thrown inside, then pushed it closed. He straightened and extended the card to her. "After you've spoken with Emma, give me a call. She's a talented student. I don't want to lose her."

And he sure as hell didn't like this misunderstanding.

She grasped the card, but he didn't release it. "What's your name?"

She hesitated. "Elizabeth."

Hawk would bet she went by Liz, but she wasn't yet friendly enough to own up to it. He released the card. "Do me a favor and let me deal with the police." She opened her mouth to reply, but he cut her off, "I'd rather you weren't on Reid's radar."

She hesitated. "What do you mean?"

"I mean, he's a mean son of a bitch who won't blink an eye at hurting you if he thinks I'll care."

She snorted. "You wouldn't care."

"I would. You'd better get home. I'll wait until you're in your car."

She stared for a moment, and he thought she would say something more, but she got out of the truck without a word.

LIZ REACHED ACROSS THE KITCHEN TABLE AND CLASPED HER daughter's hand. Last night, while Liz had paid her visit to the university, Emma had returned home sick with a cold. Liz hadn't known she was there until she'd appeared in the kitchen twenty minutes ago.

"I'm not mad," Liz said. "You're young. He's older and knows better." She recalled Professor Hawkins' cool composure when she'd accused him of sleeping with Emma. "The man is a cool character."

"What do you mean *he's a cool character*?" Emma's eyes widened. "Oh, Mom, you didn't—"

"Em, I couldn't take the chance he would use the dig as an opportunity to manipulate you."

Emma stared. "You went to my professor and accused him of screwing me?"

"*Emma*," Liz said.

Emma wiped her stuffy nose with the tissue she gripped. "I don't believe this. Professor Hawkins has never looked at me the wrong way, much less slept with me. He wouldn't go for it even if I wanted to."

"The guy is young and gorgeous," Liz said. "You're telling me he would resist a young woman like you?"

Emma shook her head. "I'm really surprised at you, Mom. If we were talking about a beautiful female professor, would you say that?"

"It's not the same," Liz said.

"Oh, my God." She rolled her eyes. "My mother is a sexist."

Liz hadn't forgotten Professor Hawkins' calm insistence that she talk to Emma, then talk to him. How many guilty men would have been so composed? She also remembered the confession that he'd thought she was a hooker. No, a "high-priced call girl." That would account for the way he'd backed her against the truck and kissed her.

Kissed her? The memory of nearly getting run over by the SUV, mingled with the recollection of his steel arms around her when he'd pulled her to safety, caused her nipples to tightened as they had last night. Which was he, letch or hero?

That question, and the memory of his hard body pressed against her, had kept her awake half the night. Was it really possible he was a hero?

"You're not protecting him?" Liz persisted.

"I know better than to sleep with my professors." Emma slumped in her chair. "I'm quitting the class."

Liz's heart twisted. "No way. He said you were a talented student. He doesn't want to lose you."

Emma eyed her doubtfully. "He said that?"

"He did."

"You're making that up so I won't be mad at you."

"Emma Louise Williams, you know I wouldn't lie."

She snorted through a stuffy nose. "I thought I knew you wouldn't accuse my professor of—"

"Emma!" Liz pinned her daughter with a hard stare. "Tell me something, young lady."

Emma groaned.

"Don't roll your eyes at me. I'm sorry. I screwed up, I admit it, but don't act like I went off half-cocked without good cause."

Em's mouth fell open. "Good cause? He's my professor. He's *old*."

"You're telling me you never noticed how gorgeous he is?" Liz demanded.

Emma's gaze sharpened. "You think he's gorgeous?"

"I'm old, not blind."

Emma rolled her eyes again. "Forty-four isn't old."

"You just said he was old. I'm ancient compared to him."

"He's old for me. Not you."

Liz blinked. "What?"

A knowing look entered her daughter's eyes. "What made you think we had a thing?"

Heat flooded Liz's cheeks. "Don't change the subject."

"You first, Mom. You made this mess."

Liz started to argue, but she was right. "I heard you on the phone."

"Eavesdropping *and* butting into my business," Emma said. "Where does it end, young lady?"

Liz narrowed her eyes. "Don't get carried away. From my end, the conversation sounded pretty incriminating. Talk of how gorgeous he is and what a great relationship you have."

"We do, as professor and student. He's an amazing teacher."

"I'm so sorry, Em, but you can't fully blame me. You were talking about how good he is in bed." Emma's mouth twisted into a disgusted look, and Liz added, "You said he was perfect."

"Perfect for you."

Liz stared. "For me? What? He's got to be at least fifteen years younger than me."

"Twelve."

"And the difference is...?"

Emma rose. "In your mind."

Chapter 3

The ring of the doorbell pulled Liz from the contract she was reviewing on her laptop. She rose and wound her way from her office at the back of the house to the front door. She looked out the window and saw two men on the stoop.

She opened the door. "Can I help you?"

"Good afternoon, ma'am," the first man said. "I'm Detective Carlisle and this is Detective Lyons. Are you Elizabeth Williams?"

Detectives. So, Professor Hawkins must have reported what happened last night, as promised.

"Yes," she said. "I'm Elizabeth Williams."

"We would like to talk to you about an incident last night at the university parking lot," Detective Carlisle said.

"Can I see your badges, please?" she asked.

Both men showed their badges.

Liz nodded and stepped aside. "Come in."

She seated them on the couch in the living room, then sat on the nearest chair.

"What can I do for you?" she asked.

Detective Carlisle said, "We have a report that a black SUV tried to run you and Professor Hawkins down in the university parking lot last night."

Liz nodded. "Yes."

Both men took out small notebooks.

"Did you get a look at the driver?" Detective Lyons asked.

Liz shook her head. "No. Their headlights blinded me before I had a chance to see anything."

"You say 'they,'" Detective Carlisle said. "Was there more than one person in the vehicle?"

"Two men," she said.

"You're sure they were men?"

"They looked larger than women."

"What were you doing at the university?" he asked.

Heat rippled through Liz at the memory of her accusations that the professor was having an affair with Emma. "My daughter is a student in Professor Hawkins class. I was there to speak with him about her."

"Really?" Detective Carlisle's gaze bore into her.

Why did she suddenly feel as if she was on trial?

"Yes. You can check with the school. But what difference does it make why I was there? I'm the one who nearly got ran over."

"Did anyone know you were going there?" Detective Lyons asked. "Is there any reason someone would want to hurt you?"

She shook her head "No. Professor Hawkins told me he believes they were men working for Vance Reid, the developer."

"Why would he do something like this?" Lyons asked.

"I guess there's some kind of dispute over land that involves Professor Hawkins," she replied. "He must have told you all this."

"You and the professor didn't have some kind of altercation?" the detective asked.

She remembered his body pressed against hers and his rough kiss, and the way he'd hugged her close when he'd saved her life by pulling her from the SUV's path.

"No," she replied.

"We have a witness who says Professor Hawkins assaulted you."

"Assaulted me?" Liz recalled threatening to report him for attempted rape. The reaction had been a bit dramatic. She'd been angry. "Your witness is mistaken."

"He didn't shove you against his truck and take liberties?" Lyons asked.

Her heart rate jumped. What was she supposed to say?

"He did not assault me in any way. What's this about?" she demanded. "I thought you were here to investigate someone trying to run us down, but you're acting as if he's the criminal. Did your witness see the SUV try to mow us down? Or the way he saved me from being hit by the SUV? The car hit Professor Hawkins' truck. Have you seen it?"

"We saw it," Detective Lyons said.

"What did your witness say about that?" she demanded.

"They saw the SUV and reported it to us immediately," he said.

"Professor Hawkins didn't report it?" she asked, then realized how bad her question made him look.

Detective Lyons nodded. "Yes, he did report the incident."

Liz relaxed a notch.

"So there's no one you know of who would threaten you?" Detective Carlisle asked.

She frowned. "I work for Leland Industries, a clothing manufacturer. Who would try to kill me?"

"You didn't recognize the men in the vehicle?" Detective Carlisle asked.

"I didn't see anything but large figures."

"Why didn't you report the incident, Ms. Williams?" Detective Lyons asked.

"Professor Hawkins advised me to go directly home. He said he would talk to you."

"Surely, you knew we would need to speak with you," the detective said.

"And here you are."

Detective Lyons held her gaze for a long moment, then flipped closed his notebook. He pulled a card from within his jacket pocket, then rose. Detective Carlisle followed suit, and Liz stood, as well.

Lyons handed her the card. "If you think of anything else, give us a call."

She took the card. "That's it?"

He looked at her. "Is there something else you can think of?"

"No."

He nodded. "If there is, don't hesitate to call."

She escorted them to the door. Lyons went out first, then Carlisle.

Carlisle paused in the doorway. "You sure there's nothing you want to report about Professor Hawkins?"

Ire flared. "Do I in any way look like an abused woman?"

"Most women don't look the part," he said.

"Maybe not to everyone, but you're a seasoned police officer," she said.

He nodded. "If you need anything, call."

"I'll do that."

They left and Liz collapsed against the door. She'd made a

real mess by visiting Professor Hawkins last night. Now she had to fix things—double time.

———

AN HOUR LATER, LIZ TURNED A BEND ON THE DIRT ROAD THAT wound through the Matatzal foothills and spotted Professor Anthony Hawkins' green Chevy parked amongst half a dozen other vehicles a quarter of a mile ahead. She slowed and turned off the road. His assistant had said he would be at the dig all day.

The driver's side of the Chevy came into view, and she hit the brakes, eyes glued to the dent in the side of the truck bed. Her stomach knotted. The eight thousand pounds of steel that had created that damage had careened across the parking lot toward her last night. If Professor Hawkins hadn't pulled her out of the way, the mammoth vehicle would have mowed her down. He'd put his life on the line to save her, despite the fact she'd accused him of seducing her daughter. And she'd mucked up things by making the police suspicious of him.

Liz willed her pounding heart to slow as she pulled the Land Cruiser to a stop beside a Subaru Forester fifty feet from where the desert floor sloped downward out of sight. The dig had to be taking place somewhere beyond the edge.

She cut the engine and gazed through the windshield at clouds that hung low over the higher peaks in the distance. A group of tall rocks, up ahead on the left, rose as if they'd speared through the Earth's surface. She had lived her entire life in Arizona and never grew tired of the stark beauty. Yellow spring wildflowers grew in spurts amongst the pale green brush, and saguaro cacti stood sentinel throughout the jagged landscape, as they had for eons.

Liz released a breath. She couldn't admire the view all day. "He asked you to talk to him after you spoke with Em," she murmured. "You owe him and Emma that much, and he deserves to know the police suspect he—" She groaned. It had been bad enough facing him to apologize about thinking he was sleeping with Emma. Now…. She reached for the keys and realized her fingers were trembling. "Get a hold of yourself. He's a young man—too young for you—and he isn't interested in you."

The admonition didn't wipe away the memory of his warm breath on her face or the way he'd almost kissed her in the truck. *Almost* was the key word. He hadn't. His rough kiss before that had been because he'd thought Vance Reid sent her to seduce him and he'd been mad as hell. A shiver sped down her arms. How did a woman go about seducing a man like him? She jarred from the thought. By being fifteen years younger, for starters.

She got out of the car and caught sight of someone before they disappeared out of sight around the large rocks. Liz slowed, suddenly unsure she could face him. She'd made fool enough of herself last night. If anyone guessed her attraction to him and word reached Emma…. Her apology could wait but warning him she'd been questioned by the police couldn't. She didn't like the idea of the two detectives showing up at the dig and accusing him of assaulting her. Or worse, leading him to believe she had told them he assaulted her.

Get it over with, she mentally ordered. *Then go home and have a strong drink.*

Liz walked to where the ground sloped and stopped. A hundred feet up ahead, half a dozen people knelt or squatted among different sections separated by twine over a tenth of an acre. Hints of three structures were visible in the earth.

Trowels, root cutters, wooden picks, shovels, and spades were scattered or in use. Mesh wire boxes were set up for sifting through dirt. She caught sight of Professor Hawkins lying on his stomach, intent on something he was carefully uncovering with a small brush.

Despite Liz's best efforts, her pulse picked up speed. Dark curls stuck out in a tousled mass below the worn felt cowboy hat he wore. His cotton shirt was rolled up to his forearms, and his long legs seemed to go on forever in tight blue jeans heavy with desert dust. His ass—good Lord, she wasn't going to be able to do this. He hadn't even looked in her direction, and already she was melting like a sixteen-year-old.

Of course, he chose that moment to look up. His gaze met hers, and he broke into a smile. Her heart stopped. She really wasn't going to get through this. He shoved to his feet and stepped over the twine. Liz started down the hill toward him, then realized she should have waited for him at the top. That would have been noncommittal. She could have said her piece, then left. But she'd started this downward spiral. Now she had to crash and burn. They met at the bottom of the incline.

"I'm relieved to see you," he said.

She blinked against the glare of the late morning sun. Why hadn't she worn sunglasses? What better way to hide?

"I've come to apologize," she said.

A corner of his mouth lifted. "No need. Emma's young to be in undergraduate school. It's a jungle. You're right to look after her."

"Thanks, but I should have talked to her before doing battle. She made that abundantly clear." Liz silently berated herself for the thousandth time. That would teach her to eavesdrop. "Emma's threatening to drop your class," she said.

"She's a smart kid. Surely, she understands your mistake?"

Liz grunted. "Oh, she understands, all right."

A question flickered across his face, and Liz cursed her big mouth when he laughed and said, "She figured out how what happened when you came to see me, huh?"

Liz nodded. "Like you said, she's a smart kid. Too smart, sometimes. But that's not all." Or the worst part, she silently added. "The police came to see me this morning."

"I expected that," he said.

"Did you know they have a witness who saw us in the parking lot?"

His brow furrowed, then understanding gleamed in his eye. "Damn."

"I'm so sorry," Liz said.

His expression hardened. "It's not your fault. I'm half guilty of what the cops think I did. I got aggressive with you. I'm sorry, Liz."

Warmth fluttered across the inside of her stomach. He *would* call her Liz, instead of Elizabeth.

"Let's forget it," she said.

He shook his head. "I'm lucky you'll talk to me at all."

"I could say the same," she said.

"No, you couldn't. It's one thing for you to think you're protecting your daughter, quite another for a man to intimidate a woman."

"You did make it up to me by saving my life." A rush of emotion flooded her. She'd never dreamed anyone would throw themselves in harm's way to save her.

His expression turned grim. "Do the cops admit to having any leads on who the guys are?"

She shook her head. "I told them you suspected Reid's men."

"I bet they didn't much care for that idea."

Liz startled. "Are you saying they don't want to catch Mr. Reid if he's guilty?"

"Vance Reid is a very powerful man around here," Hawk replied. "Even you knew who he was."

She nodded. "He built the big mall that just went up. Still, the police must want to stop him. If he's guilty."

"Maybe. Or maybe it has to be a lot worse before the right people take notice."

"What exactly is going on with him and you?" she asked. "You said he wants you to declare a dig out in Mesa to be Navajo. Why would he care?"

"The dig crosses onto property he's building on. By all indications, the site is Paleo-Indian and could predate anything we've found so far."

She grunted. "Pinning down evidence of Paleo-Indians is like hunting ghosts in a fog."

Surprise flickered across his face. "You sure you're not an archaeologist?"

Liz laughed. "Em was eight when she decided she wanted to be an archaeologist. Once she'd exhausted the library, she made me buy every book on Native American history she could find."

"I see why she's doing so well," he said.

"Listen..." Liz hesitated, "I don't have much experience with police, but the two detectives I spoke with wanted pretty badly for me to say that you..."

"Assaulted you?" he finished for her.

Liz nodded.

He released a breath. "I was wrong to blame you for Reid's actions. Even if he had sent you, that doesn't give me the right to be aggressive."

She laid a hand on his arm. "Really, it's ok. I did grab you in an effort to stop you."

He shook his head. "I don't care if you'd knocked me on my ass, it's not ok. The cops are right to make sure you weren't harmed."

She allowed her hand to fall back to her side. "I'm not harmed because you saved me."

"Professor," a young man called.

He looked over his shoulder.

"Come take a look at this," the young man said.

Professor Hawkins placed a hand on the small of Liz's back and started them forward. The warmth of his fingers penetrated the fabric of her blouse. She concentrated on taking steady steps.

"I'll talk to Emma," he said. "She doesn't have to take my class, but this is a tough field and she's doing herself a big favor by staying ahead of the game."

"What do you mean she doesn't have to take your class?" Liz asked.

"My class is a graduate course."

"Good Lord."

He looked at her. "You didn't know?"

Liz gave a soft laugh. "She left me in the dust long ago."

"You obviously did a good job with her."

"Or she did a good job with me."

He chuckled. "Don't let her know that."

They reached the young man, and Professor Hawkins dropped to a squat outside the roped off section, beside a round discoloration in the even soil where the ground had been levelled.

"A bioturbation," Liz said.

He looked up. "Very good." His attention shifted back to the ground. "Log and photograph the bioturbation, then continue digging around it. Let me know if you find any more."

The kid nodded, and the professor rose. He lightly grasped her arm and stepped several feet away from the section the young man was working.

He released her. "Did you study archaeology?"

She shook her head. "Em and I have been on several digs together."

"Sounds as if you enjoyed it."

She nodded. "I did. I'd love to do more. But these days she's so busy with school, there's not much time."

"Why not join in here?"

Liz blinked. "I—I don't know."

"Do you have any place to be?"

There had been no pressing business at Leland Industries, so she'd left her assistant manager in charge for the day. "I don't know now if I should—"

"We can always use extra help," he cut in, "and it'll give you a chance to have a little fun."

The dig was out of cell phone range, but Liz had no worries about Nancy's ability to keep production of the Linda Bellmont clothing line running on time at the factory. Still, Professor Hawkins didn't know that.

"That dress won't do," he said before she could refuse. "At least, not given the crowd we have here."

She startled. *Not given the crowd?*

"I have an extra pair of coveralls you can use, and I'm sure we can scare up a pair of sneakers or work boots. Last thing you want to do is ruin the leather on those loafers."

"I'm not an archaeologist," she insisted.

Once again, he placed a hand to the small of her back and started them walking alongside the dig. "Maybe you should become one."

"I... That's ridiculous." Her mind reeled at the feel of his hand on her back. She flushed. "I'm too old to consider a second career."

"Nonsense. You could have your degree in four years."

In four years, she would be pushing fifty.

"I would be glad to help set up your classes," he said.

Liz stumbled. His arm shot around her waist, and he yanked her against him. Her shoulder pressed against the solid wall of his chest. A mental picture rose of her breasts crushed beneath that dark expanse, her arms and legs locked around him as his cock slid in and out of her channel in full, long strokes. She jerked her gaze up to his. He stared back, dark eyes intense as if reading her thoughts. From the corner of her eye, she registered the young woman who had straightened from her kneeling position beside the middle section of the dig was staring at them.

Liz pulled free. "I, uh, I'm sorry. You're right, these shoes aren't meant for an archaeological dig."

A corner of his mouth twitched, and she narrowed her eyes in warning. He sobered and began walking again.

When they'd passed the dig and started up the incline toward the cars, he said, "I have to ask. I didn't give Emma the wrong impression, did I?"

"Wrong impression, no. It was a complete misunderstanding on my part. All me. She had no designs on you and didn't think you had designs on her," Liz added he last in a rush.

"That's a pretty big misunderstanding," he said.

Despite his casual tone, Liz had the distinct feeling the wheels inside his head were turning full steam in an effort to piece together what had happened. He couldn't possibly guess the truth. Could he?

"Chalk it up to age." She laughed.

"Age?" He slid his gaze down her body.

Her nipples tightened, and she prayed they didn't poke past her bra and against the cotton fabric of her dress.

He lifted his eyes back to her face. "If your mind is in as good a shape as your body, you can't use that excuse." She gasped in surprise, but he didn't give her a chance to say anything, and asked, "How did you come to this...misunderstanding?"

Her heart jumped into an erratic beat. "Like I said, age."

He studied her for a few seconds. "Maybe it's best I ask Emma."

"No!" Liz burst out, then quickly added, "I mean, you'll only embarrass her."

"Embarrass her? I doubt that." He lifted his brow in question.

She narrowed her eyes. Coming here had been a mistake. "I overheard a phone conversation and got it all wrong. Let's leave it at that."

"You're not playing fair, Liz."

A flush of warmth dug bone deep. He said her name with an intimacy she couldn't remember ever having heard in a man's voice. She shook her head, unable to get a word past her lips.

"What did she say?" he asked.

"I couldn't repeat it even if I wanted to."

A predatory glint lit his eyes. "Had to be pretty scandalous to get you down to the campus ready to kill me."

"You might want to be careful," she muttered. "The desire to kill you is still simmering."

His gaze bored into her. "Simmering is exactly how I want you, sweetheart. Until I get you hot."

Chapter 4

They reached the parked cars, and Hawk feared Liz would bolt. He cupped her elbow and was sure he felt the same tremor he'd detected a moment ago when he touched her. Last night's escapade had left her skittish, but he was betting the age difference was what had her worried now. He would dispel that fear soon enough.

"I'm really not sure about working on your dig," she said.

The tremble in her body had reached her voice, and he wanted like hell to bury himself in her, balls deep, and kiss her until that tremble turned into a shudder that rocked her body with orgasm.

"We could use the help," he said.

They reached his truck. Hawk stopped at the passenger side and opened the door. He glanced in the direction of the dig. From this position, they were completely out of sight of everyone. He maneuvered her between him and the door. Liz snapped her head up to meet his gaze.

"I should have an extra pair of coveralls." He leaned past her to the passenger side floorboard, and she pressed back against the edge of the seat. He grabbed the duffel from the floor, then paused and looked at her.

She stared, clearly uncertain of what his advance meant. He would have thought she had men crawling all over her. Surely, she couldn't misread his desire. Desire? Hell, this was all-out lust. He hadn't forgotten the feel of her lush body against his last night when he'd kissed her. The jolt of desire had startled him, and he'd been as close as he'd ever come to asking a woman he believed was working the wrong side of a deal to allow him to fuck her. But she wasn't with Vance Reid, so, when she did finally allowed him in her into bed, he wouldn't feel guilty about taking his time making her come again and again, then doing the same thing as often as she'd let him.

Hawk released the duffel, straightened, and traced a line down her cheek where a lock of hair moved the the whisper of breeze. "You're quite beautiful."

Her mouth parted in surprise, and the uncertainty in her gaze deepened. Hawk's grandfather swore Hawk had the supernatural sense that ran among the men in his family. Hawk hadn't put much stock in the old superstitions, but by the time he was fifteen he'd given up denying his uncanny ability to sense what other people felt.

Last night, when he'd mistaken her for a prostitute, that *ability* must have been out to lunch. Right now, however, the awareness hummed through him like a live wire that insisted Liz Williams wanted him as badly as he wanted her. The sense was also telling him she would talk herself out of her feelings for him the moment he was out of sight. He had to give her a reason not to walk away.

He leaned further into her and brushed his lips against hers. She clutched his shoulders. Heat streaked through him, hardening his cock. Hawk drew her closer, forcing back an uncharacteristic compulsion to crush her to him.

Easy, he told himself. *Make sure this time she wants you.*

He flicked his tongue against her lips. She opened for him in clear invitation. That was all he needed. Hawk swept his tongue inside, tasting, sucking, thrusting as he would inside her pussy, if she'd let him. He wanted to taste her, *all* of her.

She tentatively brushed her breasts against him, then slid a hand up the back of his neck and fisted his hair. Hawk cupped her ass and lifted her so that her mound was level with his erection. He braced her against the seat and slowly undulated his hips against her, careful to find her cleft and fit himself to the folds. Her breath caught, and he thought he would come in his jeans.

She abruptly pulled back. "Professor—"

"Hawk," he said with a hoarse laugh.

"What?"

"My friends call me Hawk."

"Hawkins," she murmured, then, "Hawk, I think—"

"No thinking, Liz."

She wiggled, and he tightened his grip on her ass.

"You don't understand," she said in a breathless voice that threatened to send him over the edge.

"I understand perfectly, sweetheart. You're worried about the age difference."

"An age difference you're not up to speed on."

"Not up to speed on?" he repeated.

He gave his heart a moment to slow, then lowered her feet back to the ground. When he leaned a shoulder against the door frame and crossed his arms over his chest, her gaze followed the action, then jerked back up to his face. His cock pulsed. Yeah, she wanted him.

"Fill me in on what I'm missing," he said.

She hesitated. "I'm not forty."

"So you said last night."

"Try forty-four."

He tried not to laugh. "Is this where I'm supposed to look shocked?"

"Twelve years is a huge span," she said.

"Twelve years?" he repeated. "Who told you my age?"

Startlement flickered in her eyes, and he realized he'd caught her. "That's what you overheard Emma talking about, wasn't it? What did she say, Liz? How good-looking I was, what a good lay I was? How perfect I might be for her mother?"

"No," Liz snapped. "If she'd said that, I wouldn't have made a fool of myself at the school."

He gave a slow nod. "But she said it when you spoke with her afterwards, didn't she?"

Liz's gaze flicked past him, and he knew she was gauging a dash for her car.

Hawk wrapped his arms around her and she allowed him to draw her close. "Are a few years age difference going to stop you from getting to know me?" he asked.

"A few years?" she sputtered.

"Statistics say women outlive men by ten years. Women don't even reach their sexual peak until their forties, then they stay there for decades."

Her eyes narrowed. "You're making that up."

"Am I? Look at you, sweetheart. Your body is humming. You're a wet dream come to life."

"I—I am not," she breathed in a voice that only proved his point.

He cut off any further response with a kiss. Her mouth

moved beneath his in a half-hearted attempt to continue the argument, but he slipped his tongue past her lips. She arched into him, and he groaned. Hawk lifted her onto the seat and stepped closer so that his dick pressed flush against the juncture between her legs. He cupped a breast and kneaded the flesh through the thin layer of her dress.

Hawk slid a wet kiss down her cheek to her neck. The sun had brought out a taste of salt and desire. Her head fell back, and he continued downward to the V-neck of her dress. He swiped his tongue between the fabric and her skin, then along the luxurious velvet rise of her full breast. She squirmed, and he loosened his crushing hug and coaxed her arms around him. God, how he wanted those arms and her long legs wrapped tight around him when he pistoned into her. They would both come hard. He slipped a hand under her dress.

Her head snapped up. "Someone will see."

"They're too absorbed in the dig." He kissed her breast through the fabric.

"You can't be sure," she insisted.

He kissed the other nipple. "I know these students. They won't come up for air...until I do."

Her mouth parted in a silent gasp.

"Trust me." He slipped a finger between her lace panties and curls.

Liz gasped. What was she doing? Exactly what she'd sworn she wouldn't do—throwing herself at her daughter's young professor.

Because you trust him. Liz startled at the unexpected thought.

He bent his head to the spot where her neck met shoulder. His warm breath washed across the sensitive spot he gently nibbled. Her senses blurred. He slid a finger beneath her panties and into her folds. Liz clamped her legs together. Her thighs tightened around his waist, and her mind registered the throb of her clit against his rigid length. She reflexively pulled back, but he grasped a thigh, keeping her tight against him.

"No." His hoarse whisper sent a shiver through her.

Liz remained stock still at the feel of the long digit that played at the entrance to her channel.

"You're so wet," he murmured.

He slipped his finger inside. The invasion caught her off guard, then pleasure followed hard and fast. She gulped air. His finger slid in and out. Desire raged through her. His head dipped, and he sucked a nipple through her cotton dress. Tiny tendrils of pleasure spiked from the sensitive bud. He thrust harder. Her mind muddled. She should stop him. Her heart pounded. Liz braced her hands on the seat behind her and pulsed into his finger.

He released her nipple, then pressed his mouth to her ear. "That's it, sweetheart."

Heat rocketed through her at the sound of his deep voice. Her clit tightened. *God.* She was close. Hawk pulled her skirt waist-high, and Liz jerked her head up to see him staring at his finger moving in and out, eyes dark with lust. He yanked his finger out. She jolted with the sudden loss, but he dropped to a squat before she could respond, yanked aside, and covered her with his mouth.

His tongue swept up through her folds. She swallowed a groan. He parted her swollen lips wide and closed his mouth around her clit, then sucked. Liz trembled, eyes glued to him as he drew on her nub harder. Pleasure crashed through her from the inside out. She couldn't prevent a cry and clamped her legs tight around his head. He didn't miss a beat, his sucking rhythm pulling, pulling, pulling until she spiraled out of control. Orgasm burst through her. Her body clenched. Liz drove her fingers into his dark hair as a second spasm rocked her, then a third, smaller orgasm tightened her body before relaxing.

Pleasure subsided. He gently kissed her, licked, and kissed again, then straightened her panties and tugged her dress down over her legs. He stood and hugged her close. Liz collapsed into his embrace without resistance. Hawk's arms tightened around her, and she breathed deep of his earthy scent, immensely glad for the comforting warmth. Then embarrassment heated her cheeks. How could she look him in the eye? What about Emma?

Liz groaned and straightened from him. "I'm so sorry."

"I'm sure as hell not." He released her and draped an elbow over the open window. "I'll do that again the first chance you give me—and more."

She tried not to fidget, despite the remnants of pleasure between her thighs. "This shouldn't have happened in the first place. And on the side of the road, for God's sake. It can't happen again."

"Nonsense." He grasped her chin with two fingers. "You'll get over the embarrassment soon enough." A corner of his mouth lifted in a smile that sent butterflies skittering across her stomach. "I promise."

"Professor—"

"Hawk," he corrected. "You can't think of calling me 'Professor' after that." He gave the side of her leg a gentle pat. "Get up."

She rose on unsteady legs, and he reached for the duffel.

He set the bag on the seat and pulled a pair of grey coveralls from inside. "Let's get these on you and do a little digging."

Liz glanced in the direction of the dig. "Really, is that a good idea?"

"The best I've had all day." He dropped a kiss on her cheek, then lifted his brows. "Almost."

Chapter 5

Liz lay with her stomach to the ground, digging inch by inch in a twenty-four by twenty-four inch plot. The tedious work allowed her mind to replay *and replay* what had happened between her and Hawk, and she couldn't deny why she'd done it—or how badly she wanted a repeat performance. He'd risked his life for hers, a possibility not every woman got the opportunity to test, and he was honest. Package that in six feet of bronzed steel, and she hadn't stood a chance. Coming here had been a huge mistake.

A shadow fell across her, and she glanced up. Hawk stood over her.

"Lunchtime." He lifted a soft-cover cooler. "I'll share."

The sun glared behind him in a blaze of orange that emphasized his angular face and the patch of tanned chest visible above the open collar of his white shirt. Her pulse skipped a beat. She had to quit now while she still had the ability to do so. He bent, and Liz glimpsed determination in his eyes as he grasped her arm. Awareness jumpstarted her heart when his fingers tightened around her arm and he pulled her up. He kept a light but firm hold as she stepped over the twine that separated the dig from the rest of the desert. Liz glanced at the students who sat cross-legged in the shade of the nearest pillar. They were absorbed in food and each other.

"Hawk," she began.

"Over here," he interrupted.

Liz sighed and allowed him to lead her to the pillars on the opposite side of the small compound. He stopped within the broad strips of shade cast by the cluster of large stones.

She halted. "I really think I should go."

"It's lunch, Liz. What do you expect to happen?"

Her cheeks warmed, but she managed to arch a brow.

He laughed. "Fair enough. But you can relax. As much as I'd like to pick up where we left off, I won't touch you in plain view of the students."

Her stomach gelled. There was no missing the implication that, once they were out of sight, he *would* touch her again. He gently urged her to sit, and she complied, as much out of a desire not to embarrass herself as the fact that she feared her legs would give way. Hawk sat beside her. He opened the cooler and pulled out a napkin, then laid bottled water, barbecued chicken, cornbread, fresh tomatoes, and chocolate chip cookies on the cloth.

"You do come prepared," she said.

He grinned. "A man gets hungry out here."

"So does a woman," she had to admit.

"I didn't bring plates," he said. "Just dig in with your fingers."

She opened a bottle of water, dribbled a few drops on her hands, then wiped them on the dusty coveralls, only to have the dust turn muddy.

"You spend enough time out here, and you'll have dust in your veins instead of blood," Hawk said.

Liz grimaced. "I think I'm halfway there." She grabbed a chicken leg, then leaned back against the rock and bit into the meat. The tang of the barbecue sauce burst across her tongue. "Perfect."

He nodded. "Nothing better than cold barbecue."

They ate in silence for a few minutes before Liz said, "I'm surprised you're in the field. Isn't bioarcheology conducted in a lab?"

Hawk took a swig of water and washed down the ample slice of cornbread he'd eaten. "It is. But this is where it all begins." He stretched out his legs and crossed ankle over ankle. "You can't know the material you're analyzing until you see where it comes from, feel the dirt on your fingers." He lifted a hand and looked at his dark fingers. "And beneath your fingernails." He released a slow breath, his gaze on the desert that stretched out before them. "There's nothing like being out here." His eyes shifted to her. "Plus, I like getting dirty."

Liz startled, then snorted. "Very funny. What got you into archaeology?"

He dug a thigh from the plastic tub. "Two pieces of damned good luck." He bit into the chicken.

"What do you mean?" she asked, then took another bite of her chicken.

"A history teacher and one tenacious ASU archaeology professor. Not many kids who grow up on reservations make it into graduate programs."

Mortification warmed her cheeks. "Hawk, I—"

He shook his head. "You didn't say anything wrong."

"I didn't even think about it," she said.

"That's not a bad thing—not totally. You didn't stereotype me."

"Who could possibly stereotype *you*?"

He chuckled. "I guess they don't know me the way you do."

This time, heat pooled between her legs and tugged hard.

He took another bite of chicken. "What about you? What do you do?"

"I manage a clothing manufacturing plant."

His brows rose. "Tough job."

She thought of the phone call she would have to make tomorrow to GFW Industries if they forestalled the payment due to Leland Industries, and laughed. "It has its moments." Liz grimaced. "But I'm much more boring than you are."

"You're anything but boring, sweetheart." Fire burned in his eyes.

Her heart skipped. "I...I... Stop looking at me like that."

"I plan to do a lot more than look, first chance I get."

"You promised to be good," she whispered.

"You're sitting twelve inches from me, Liz. I am being good."

"Your students don't have to hear us to guess what we're talking about," she said. "It's written all over your face, for God's sake."

"There's plenty of privacy on the other side of that southwest pillar," he replied matter-of-factly.

She gaped. "You're incorrigible."

"I'm a helluva lot more than that."

Damn him, he was. She grabbed her water and took a long swig.

"You must want me bad to need that water," he said.

She choked, then spewed water. Water sucked down her windpipe. She wheezed.

Hawk gave her a hearty slap on the back. "You okay?"

Her vision blurred, but she still discerned the amusement *and* satisfaction in his eyes. Liz opened her mouth to tell him to take a flying leap. Instead, she dragged in another harsh breath.

"Breathe easy," he coaxed.

She shot him a dark look.

"It's not my fault." He rubbed gentle circles on her back.

The constriction in her throat eased. She took a small sip of water and was rewarded with a cooling sensation on the way down. She released a breath and wiped at the moisture in the corners of her eyes.

"Next time, take it easy with the water," he said.

"Next time, I'll take you over my knee."

His mouth twitched into a smile. "Promise?"

Liz groaned, tore a hunk off the chicken leg with her teeth, and wondered what it would be like to do the same to him.

***

SUNLIGHT SKIMMED THE DISTANT EDGE OF THE DESERT WHEN LIZ looked up from where she lay brushing loose dirt from the hard ground. Nearby, Hawk gave instructions to the last two remaining students, and Liz knew what she'd known for the last two hours—she'd stayed too long.

"I'll see you here, tomorrow after class," he said to the girl. "You're in charge until I get here, Katie."

The girl nodded, and she, along with the young man standing beside her, turned and headed toward the cars. Hawk faced Liz as she rose from where she'd given a final few brush strokes to the section of dirt she'd been working on.

"Not so much as an arrowhead," she said.

He laughed. "Such is the life of an archaeologist. Ninety-eight per cent of the ground we dig doesn't yield anything."

Liz shook her head "The digs Em and I went on always yielded something."

"You were paying customers." Hawk grasped her arm and squeezed. "I promise to make up for all your hard work." He winked.

She couldn't help a laugh. He looked like a big kid. Liz sobered. That was exactly what he was. But she'd left that stage of life behind long ago.

"Listen, Hawk—"

"Here it is," he cut in. "You've had all day to conjure up reasons not to see me."

She shrugged. "It was inevitable."

"Just as this is inevitable." His fingers tightened on her flesh and he gently drew her to him.

"Hawk," she managed before his mouth lowered onto hers.

His moist lips pressed against hers sent Liz into a tailspin. Just as she'd known it would. He was right; she wanted him. But he was also right in that she'd had all day to own up to why nothing could happen between them.

Liz broke the kiss, breathing hard, and leaned her head against his chest. The hard thump of his heart made her want to listen to the sound until past dawn. A short, torrid affair would do her good. But damn it, even if Hawk was capable of separating their relationship from his relationship with Emma, when things went bad, Emma wouldn't be. And a friend like Professor Anthony Hawkins could make all the difference to her success.

"You are a powerful temptation," Liz said through a shaky breath.

A strangled laugh broke from him. "Only a temptation? That doesn't even come close to what you are to me."

She lifted her head and met his gaze. "I've never let my personal life interfere with Emma's well-being—until today. I can't let it happen again."

"What do you expect to happen?" he asked.

"I expect explosive sex, then just as explosive a breakup."

A corner of his mouth twitched into a smile. "I scared you with that kiss last night, didn't I? And probably my driving, too?"

Liz blinked, then laughed. "Last night was...unusual but, no." She couldn't resist tracing a finger along his jaw. "You saved my life, and you didn't have to do that."

His eyes darkened. "God damn it, Liz, talk to me in that voice, and you drive me out of my mind."

Her insides liquefied. They stared at each other for a long moment before she stepped back.

"Do you really think I'm incapable of separating my personal life from my professional life?" he asked.

"I think you haven't been tested like this. Have you ever been involved with a student's mother?" Regret rolled over her. If he said yes, if she wasn't the first mother whose panties he'd got into with little resistance...

"No," he replied.

Relief gave way to reality. "Then you can't know what you'll do."

"Have you ever had a relationship with a younger man?" he asked.

She shot him a withering look.

"I'm not a child, Liz."

Her stomach did a flip. That voice didn't belong to a child. Neither did the determination and desire in his eyes.

"I'm not an asshole either," he added.

"Can you blame me for wanting to protect Emma?" she asked.

"I can blame you for using her as an excuse."

"An excuse?" She frowned. "You're out of your mind."

"You said that last night. Yet, here you are." Before she could reply he added, "Just because I haven't been involved with a student's mother, doesn't mean I haven't been *tested,* and in the toughest way a man can be tested."

Liz frowned in confusion.

"Marriage."

She blinked. "You're married?"

"Was," he said. "I told you I'm not an asshole. We're divorced."

"Divorced? What woman would divorce you?" The words were out of her mouth before she realized it.

"I divorced her." Hawk grinned. "But I like the way you think."

Liz wasn't sure whether to feel wariness or just plain curiosity. Curiosity won out. "Why did you divorce her?"

"Let's just say I took fidelity more seriously than she did."

This time, Liz couldn't stop her mouth from falling open. "I don't believe you."

He lifted a brow. "Are you saying women are incapable of being unfaithful, or is it that men are incapable of being faithful?"

What woman in her right mind would look at another man with him around? How could she possibly have the energy? The glimpse Liz had gotten of his character said he was a good man, and his lovemaking.... What had been wrong with his wife?

Liz gave him a soft smile. "I'm saying I'm sorry. Divorce is a terrible thing."

He shrugged. "Sometimes it beats the alternative."

The words were lighthearted, but Liz didn't miss the hint of pain.

"What about you?" he asked.

"Me?"

"Emma's father?"

Liz grimaced inwardly. Turnabout was fair play.

"He left when she was three," she said.

Hawk frowned. "That's it?"

"That's it. He decided a wife and a child weren't what he wanted."

Disbelief crossed Hawk's expression, then he snorted in disgust. "He discovered that a little too late. I'm sorry, Liz."

She smiled. "Sounds like we're both sorry."

His mood didn't lighten. "Maybe, but your husband had a daughter to consider. I can deal with the fallout of my mistake. Kids change everything."

Her heart warmed. He would make a good father. When that time came, he would understand. "A mother doesn't sleep with her daughter's professor," she said in a quiet voice.

A smile touched his mouth. "Dinner. That's all I'm asking."

"No, it's not."

"I didn't say I wouldn't take more," he said with startling honesty. "Hell, look at you. What man would turn you down? But what I'm saying is, I'll settle for dinner—tonight."

"It won't end there, and you know it," she said.

He studied her. "Sounds to me like it's *you* who doesn't think it can't end there."

Liz racked her brain for a response, but he saved her from the embarrassment of an answer he was sure to see straight through.

"Come on." He started them toward the rise. "It's getting dark. Let's get back to town. I know this great place." She started to argue, but he said, "Don't worry. It's an overly crowded cantina on the west side. There isn't a private corner in the place where I could get my hands between your legs."

Butterflies leapt into a riotous dance inside her stomach at the memory of his hands between her legs, his mouth.... How would she get through dinner without begging him to do that to her again?

Chapter 6

Hawk walked alongside Liz as they crested the rise. The instant before Hawk caught sight of the two flat tires on the Land Cruiser, he sensed something was wrong. Liz gasped, and he grasped her arm, bringing them to a stop.

Hawk cursed. How had he missed hearing a vehicle pull up to their cars after the kids had left? Easy. He'd been so focused on Liz that a Mack truck could have rumbled past, and he would have missed it. He scanned the area. The Chevy sat parked twenty feet beyond the Cruiser. No other cars were within view of the old road or the desert beyond. It was unlikely anyone would be hiding around the cars, but who the hell knew what these crazy assholes would do?

He dropped to a squat and looked beneath the Land Cruiser, then across the open space to the truck. No one hid beneath the two vehicles, and the truck's four tires were okay. He didn't like that. Whatever they'd done to the old Chevy wasn't obvious, which probably meant the slashed tires were an afterthought. An afterthought motivated by a reason he felt certain he wouldn't like. Hawk rose and started to tell Liz to stay put while he investigated, then realized, if anyone came up over the slope while he was at the cars, he couldn't get to her before they did.

"Come on." He started them forward. When they reached within twenty feet of the Toyota, Hawk stopped. "Wait here."

"But—"

"Let me take a look," he ordered.

Her lips pursed, but she nodded.

"Don't move," he emphasized.

"I promise."

He handed her the cooler he carried and silently cursed the worth of her promise and depth of his stupidity. After he'd delivered her safely home, he planned to find Vance Reid and beat him senseless.

Hawk approached the Land Cruiser. He looked inside, found nothing, then went around the truck and looked inside the cab. As expected, empty. He finally motioned Liz forward, then strode back to her car, where he squatted beside the front tire and ran his fingers along the gouge on the lower section of the rubber where it had been slashed with a knife.

Liz set the cooler on the ground and knelt beside him. "My God." She touched the hole, her long, slim fingers pale against the dark rubber.

"Yeah." Hawk rose and went back to his truck.

He opened the hood and scanned the engine. Nothing obvious was out of place. He knelt on one knee, braced a palm on the ground, and looked under the car. A dark circle stained the desert floor beside the passenger-side tire. He lowered himself onto his back and scooted under the truck near the stain. As suspected, fluid dripped from a cut brake line. Hawk grasped the fender, pulled himself out, and stood.

"What do you think happened?" she asked.

He considered lying, but she wouldn't be fooled by a

sugar-coated answer. Only he didn't have to tell her that her slashed tires were a message concerning her. His only living family was his grandfather who lived on the reservation. Vance Reid didn't have a big enough army to get to him there, and Hawk's friends could take care of themselves as well as he could. Hawk's jaw tensed. He'd finally given Reid what he'd been after for the last three months, a way to get at him.

"They cut my brakes and slashed your tires," Hawk said.

"Your brakes?" she burst out.

"Did you bring a cell phone?" he asked.

"Sure. But there's no service out here."

"Let's take a look."

He followed her to the Land Cruiser.

She opened the driver's side back door, then swung to face him. "My purse is gone."

Hawk nodded. "I would have been surprised if they'd left it."

"You don't have a cell phone?" she asked.

"I hate the things."

She looked nonplussed. "You're kidding."

"I used to have one and couldn't get a damn bit of work done on a dig."

She glanced around. "Why do all this then leave? That doesn't make sense."

But it did. It made more sense than anything else they'd done so far.

Panic rose like a tsunami in Liz's belly.

Get a grip, she mentally ordered. But the command didn't stop the tremble that rocketed through her body.

Hawk pulled her close, and she allowed herself to relax

against his solid body. The steady beat of his heart lulled her rampant pulse into a manageable rhythm as he stroked her hair. Tears threatened, but she bit down on her lip. The last thing he needed was a hysterical female. And she had no intention of giving Vance Reid the satisfaction of reducing her to a blubbering mass.

Liz wrapped her arms around Hawk and released a slow breath. A stirring against her abdomen confused her for a second before she realized the growing bulge would be a full-blown erection in seconds.

She straightened and looked up at him. "How can you possibly want to...."

He gave a half laugh. "It's not difficult with you, sweet-heart, but we'll save it for later." One hand slid around her neck while the other held her tight. He pressed a chaste kiss against her forehead, then pulled back. "I'll make this up to you when we get home."

Her stomach flipped, and she could only nod.

Hawk released her. "It's fifteen miles back to Highway 87, too far to walk on this old road at night." He glanced east. "Even with a full moon on the way." His gaze came back around and locked with hers. "You game for a night under the stars?"

Her heart did a double take, but to her surprise she read only concern in his eyes. That made her legs gel even more. A night under the stars with a Native American warrior who intended to protect her? Who was going to save her from him?

"What time will your students return tomorrow?" she asked.

"Katie will be here by nine a.m."

"That's not too bad," Liz said. "Emma will be worried

sick, but there's nothing I can do about it. I'm sure Katie will have a phone." She gave him a recriminating look.

He shrugged. "This'll teach me."

"What time is it?" she asked.

He glanced at his digital watch. "Seven-thirty."

"Maybe we'll get lucky, and Katie will be early."

He nodded, but she couldn't help feeling she'd be a lot luckier if Katie were late.

"Where did you leave the cooler?" he asked. "We've got plenty of food and water left."

"The other side of the car," she replied in a voice that, thankfully, didn't crack. Liz fetched the cooler, then crossed to the truck, where Hawk was retrieving a sleeping bag and blue jean jacket from behind the seat.

"You really come prepared," she said.

"The desert gets down in the forties this time of year. Without a coat and water, a person can be in trouble before you know it." He looked over his shoulder at her. "We'll be all right."

The knot in her stomach tightened when he pulled a rifle from behind the seat. Hawk shut the door and faced her.

"Were you expecting trouble?" she asked.

"I always keep a rifle on a dig. There's not much danger with a big group like today, but I spend a lot of time on digs alone. Mountain lions can be aggressive." He extended his hand in invitation. "The Toyota will be more comfortable than my truck. We can put the backseat down."

She entwined her fingers in his, and he led her toward the Land Cruiser. The casual clasp of his fingers, warm and sure, sent a frisson of awareness through her. Had it been so long that any touch from a man was so noticeable? She had to get a grip. It would be easy to get carried away with a middle-aged fantasy that ended up making a fool of her—and getting her *and* Emma hurt. Hawk had made it clear he wanted her, but he was grown up enough to put aside his sexual advances. They had to get through this night and get safely home tomorrow.

Five minutes later, Hawk had the seat down and the sleeping bag spread out across the Toyota bed. He motioned Liz in, and she ignored the idea that he was watching her rear end as she crawled inside.

"Why leave us here like this?" she asked as he closed the door behind him.

He scooted back to where she sat. "Another warning."

He stretched out kitty-corner on the sleeping bag and pulled her against his chest. The moon that lifted over the orange tinged horizon joined forces with the scent of earth and the unique masculine smell that was Hawk, and her stomach tightened with burgeoning desire. The arm wrapped around her lay heavy across her waist. A quiver radiated through her insides. Liz willed herself not to melt against the muscled expanse pressed close to her breast.

"This is low-key compared to last night's warning," she said, in a voice she prayed didn't give away the desire that throbbed between her legs with every beat of her heart. He was silent, and she was sure he could feel her nipples hardening against his chest. How long could she resist before she kissed him? "I meant what I said. I'm not going to risk Emma's relationship with you," she said.

"Nothing that happens between us will change my mind about being her advisor," he said.

"What?" Liz shoved up onto an elbow so they made eye contact in the dusky moonlight. "You're going to be her advisor?"

"She didn't tell you?"

Liz shook her head. It was like Emma not to tell her.

Emma would give up his support before hurting her. Liz hadn't considered the possibility that Emma would find a professor willing to advise her so early in her education. Her throat tightened. Emma's upset hadn't just been teenage embarrassment. Had she already gone too far?

"This is too big for me to jeopardize," she said.

"The only person who can jeopardize Emma is herself," he said, "and that's only if she doesn't do the work. I can't see her doing that."

"When things end between you and I end, you might feel differently."

"You've already made up your mind?" he asked.

"You have to admit, chances of a long-term relationship between us are slim."

"I've seen worse odds."

Liz nodded. "Maybe, but I'm not willing to gamble with my daughter's future."

He laughed. "You have nothing to say about it, sweetheart. It's a done deal."

"What do you mean?" she demanded.

"I've already assigned her senior classes."

Liz stared. "But she's only an undergrad."

"An immensely talented undergrad who deserves as much help as she can get."

"You could still change your mind."

His brows rose. "If you piss me off?"

"Wouldn't be the first time something like that has happened," she said.

"It would be a first for me. Not to mention, I'm not stupid enough to let a student's mother get between me and some great funding."

Liz blinked. "She'll garner that much funding for you?"

Hawk shrugged. "She's a hot commodity. I'm simply a

smart enough businessman to have closedd the deal before someone else did, and I have no intentions of giving her up, no matter how hard you try to talk me out of it. Though I won't stop you from plying me with your womanly wiles in order to try."

"Talk you out of it? I...I don't know how to thank you."

"I didn't do it for you, Liz. Much as I'd like to take the credit."

"I know." She swallowed the lump that had risen in her throat. "Which only makes it all the more amazing. You did it because you're a nice person."

"Mostly a good businessman," he said.

She touched his cheek. "No. A nice person."

"Careful, Liz."

A quiver rocked her stomach. The husky note in his voice would do her in. "You were right," she said.

"What?"

"I have lousy timing." Not to mention, she had mush for a brain.

He laughed and pulled her close. "Yeah, but my timing's great."

Liz thought about his *great timing* that morning when he'd had his mouth between her legs, and her pulse skipped a beat, then faltered.

"Oh, my God." She buried her head in his chest.

"What's wrong?" he demanded.

"They were watching us when you and I—" She groaned.

"They?" He chuckled, then gave her a reassuring hug. "It's more likely Reid's men came later."

"You can't know that."

"Any more than you can know they were watching," he said. "And, even if they were, the only thing they saw was us kissing."

"And you on your knees when you—" Her cheeks heated, despite knowing he couldn't see her face.

"When I what?"

His deep voice reverberated through her.

"You know what you did." She winced at the squeak in her voice.

"I can't wait to do it again."

Liz jumped at the feel of lazy circles travelling along her arm.

"You want me to touch you that way again," he said. "No woman reacts the way you did and doesn't want to have that done to her again." He brought his mouth close to her ear. "And again."

Liz had thought that very thing, and her body ached painfully at the idea.

"How do you plan on dealing with Vance Reid?" she said

The lazy circles stopped. A long stretch of silence passed between them before he said, "I'll have to make the police understand they have to step things up on their investigation."

"I don't think you're being honest," she said.

"No?"

"I think you intend to speak with him yourself."

"I would like a face-to-face," he admitted.

Liz settled her cheek more comfortably against his chest and stared through the window at the moon that rose against a darkening sky. "Do you believe he'll blink first?"

He squeezed her arm. "I was wrong to play that game with you in the truck last night. My grandfather told me my temper would get the best of me one day."

Warmth flowed like liquid silver up her arm from where he touched her.

"Reid isn't chancing that we'll beat him," Hawk said. "And I do plan to beat him. Did plan to beat him."

"Did?" Liz pushed up and met his gaze. "Now, wait a minute. You can't make any changes on my account."

He tweaked a lock of her hair. "Sweetheart, I wouldn't be able to *not* make changes if I tried."

"You *are* out of your mind. I don't know how your generation does things—"

"My generation?" His rich laughter slid across her senses like black velvet. "You're going to be able to get away with that line for about two seconds, then I'll toss you on your back and make love to you until you forget your age, your name...." His voice deepened. "But you sure as hell won't forget my name."

Chapter 7

Liz didn't resist as Hawk pulled her closer. His lips touched hers, and fire exploded between her legs. A moan slipped from her. He grasped her hips and lifted her onto his body. Her curves molded to his sharper contours, especially the rock-hard erection that dug into her abdomen.

Her head whirled. She told herself to stop, but the command evaporated with the feel of his fingers pressing into her butt and the undulation of his cock against her mound. Desire streaked through her like a runaway train—headed for a cliff. He might have been an honorable man who wouldn't let their relationship affect Emma, but he was still twelve years younger than her. She was going to crash and burn in a blaze that left nothing but ash in its wake. Liz broke the kiss and dropped her head onto his neck.

"I've wanted to do that all day," he said. "And this." He rolled, and she found herself pinned beneath him.

Air rushed from her lungs, and she gasped at the steely weight that bore down on her. She couldn't breathe. Couldn't think. She wanted to run away and stay at the same time. She grasped his shoulders in an effort to stop the spin that threatened to toss her stomach into her throat. He covered her breast with a warm palm. She shivered. He kissed her.

His tongue flicked against her mouth. Liz opened, and he drove his tongue inside, sliding along hers in languid strokes that heated her core to the boiling point. She envisioned yanking open the front of his jeans and seizing the raging cock that pressed into her belly. She wanted to touch him. *All of him.* He slid kisses across her cheek to her ear. Warm breath tickled the sensitive lobe.

"I want to fuck you hard and fast," he growled. "I'm going to make you come so hard your eyes roll back in your head." He bit down on her lobe and nibbled.

Liz drew in a sharp breath. Hawk slid off her and began unbuttoning her coveralls. Panic rushed to the surface. The full moon acted like a bright streetlamp. He was about to see her—all of her—and she was *not* at her best. What would be her best? What would be good enough for a Native American warrior?

"I—I've been working in the dirt all day." The words sounded stupid. He'd got the buttons undone clear to her waist. "I'm a mess," she insisted.

He spread the coveralls. Cool air wafted over the rise of breasts not covered by the black lace of her bra.

"The most beautiful mess I've ever seen," he murmured.

Her heart pounded as he slipped aside the bra cup and the nipple pebbled under his intense scrutiny. Hawk lifted her shoulder, eased back the coveralls, then did the same for the other shoulder. He tugged the sleeves free of her arms and dragged the coveralls downward. Liz lifted her hips, allowing the fabric to slip free, and tried to still the tremble that threatened to become a seismic disaster.

His head dipped and warm lips closed around her areola.

Pleasure strung taut between nipple and pussy. He cupped her mound with his palm. Liz whimpered. She wanted him inside her. *Now.* Needed to feel his shaft fill her balls-deep, stroke her, push her to the mind-bending orgasm he'd promised. His finger slipped between the thong and her flesh. Her clit tightened in anticipation. She pulsed against the long digit. Tiny licks of pleasure stretched out from her core.

"Hawk," she breathed.

He pressed close to her side, and she became aware of the heavy jeans that separated his cock from her naked thigh. With trembling fingers, she reached between them and grasped the top jeans' button. The sucking on her breast stilled. She froze.

"Don't stop," he murmured against her breast.

Liz shifted her gaze to the sliver of moonlight that fell across the space between them and worked free the buttons. She shoved the shirt tail up and out of the way, then pulled back the front of his jeans. A large bulge pressed against white boxer briefs. Her mouth went dry. It had been three years since she'd had a man, and *forever* since she'd had a man like Hawk. She grasped the waistband and gingerly pulled the fabric past his shaft.

His long, thick cock sprang free, aimed directly at her abdomen. Heart pounding, Liz wrapped a hand around the girth. He pulsed between her fingers. Excitement swelled on a rising tide through her. He felt so good, so hard...so male. It had been too long since she'd touched a man. Just as it had been too long since she'd tasted one. What would he do if she took him in her mouth?

Before she could talk herself out of it, Liz shoved him onto his back. She brought her face to his rod, and he remained motionless as she grasped the root and ran her tongue around the tip.

A growl reverberated from his chest, and he tunneled his fingers into her hair. Liz quelled the nervous tightening in her stomach and took him into her mouth. He thrust inside, slowly, gently, letting her set the rhythm. She resisted the urge to close her eyes and watched his length disappear inside her mouth, then reappear as she pulled back. She hollowed her cheeks, caressing the velvet steel while sucking hard on the upstroke.

His fingers tightened in her hair. "Liz."

The word came out a hoarse groan, and she was startled at the realization that she was driving him over the edge—and with little effort. She increased her rhythm. To her shock, his cock hardened further. She breathed deep, reveling in the male scent, the feel of his engorged staff filling her mouth. He'd said he would make her come so hard she saw stars. She wanted to make him come so hard he wouldn't soon forget this night, or Liz Williams. She sucked more of his length, swirling her tongue around the root.

He abruptly seized her shoulders, and she found herself on her back, him over her. He kissed her—long, hard, and demanding—then broke away and shucked his shirt, jeans, and boots. He pulled something from the back pocket of his jeans. She heard the quiet tear of paper, then he reached toward his erection, and she realized it had been a condom he'd pulled from his pocket and he was fitting it to his cock.

Suddenly, Liz felt like a fool. "Do you carry condoms around in your pocket?"

His head jerked in her direction. A heartbeat of silence passed before he said "About six months ago, I was involved with a woman. Our schedules didn't mesh, and I didn't like not being prepared. When you showed up here today, I prayed to every Native American god I know I still had one in the glove box." She heard the sheepish note in his voice. "I could have gotten creative, but I want to be inside you so badly it hurts."

In the next second, he was over her again, kissing her with a passion that had her head spinning. His weight crushed her breasts with exquisite discomfort, marbling her nipples against his smooth flesh.

"Do you want me as badly as I want you?" he murmured against her lips.

Her clit throbbed with a need unlike any she'd ever experienced. Her fantasies during those hours of digging were dim versions of the reality. Yes, she wanted him. Liz answered by shoving a hand between them and grasping his erection.

Hawk pushed onto his elbows and allowed her to position his cock at her opening. Slowly, he eased inside so that only the tip stretched her tight channel. Then he stopped and lifted his head to meet her gaze. His features were hidden in shadows against the moon that watched from beyond the window, its darkened valleys eyes that stared like a lewd voyeur. He lowered his weight onto her, cupped her face, and kissed her with a gentleness that nearly brought tears. He eased deeper. Pleasure trickled through her at the feel of the invasion. She gripped his shoulders.

He stilled. "You all right?"

She slid a hand up and threaded her fingers through the hair at his nape. "Don't stop."

He gave a gravelly laugh and surged hilt deep. She cried out and dug her fingers into his flesh. He eased out, then in again. She lifted her legs, bracing her feet on the car floor, and raised her hips to meet his slow thrusts. Hawk trailed hot licks down her neck. Sizzles skittered across her flesh. She shivered, her fingers tightening in his hair.

"That's it, sweetheart." He thrust hard.

She gasped at the pleasure that rocketed through her.

"You like that?" he asked.

Liz pulled his mouth to hers. He increased the speed of his thrusts. She wrapped her legs around his waist. A tickle began in her core. Her heart jumped into warp speed. Harder, deeper, he drove into her. Emotion tightened her chest. His pubic bone bumped her pleasure point. Pleasure ripped through her. She angled her hips for more direct contact. He drove deeper, harder. His head rammed into her cervix. Her clit tightened, and she cried out in her release.

"Fuck," Hawk muttered.

His arms slid beneath her, crushing her as he pounded into her. She couldn't think. A second orgasm crashed over her. Her channel walls tightened around his cock. His hoarse groan pierced the desire that blanketed her brain. He pumped faster, his breath coming in labored gasps in her ear until he threw his head back, muscles straining with his climax. Liz arched into him, and he growled, thrust deep twice more, then collapsed on top of her, heart thundering so hard she felt the powerful beat against her breast.

Hawk slid to her side and hugged her close. "Give me five minutes, sweetheart, and we'll do that again."

Chapter 8

Hawk's eyes snapped open. Awareness danced across his nerves. He pushed onto an elbow and peered through the window at the road. Headlights cut across the night a mile up the road. This wasn't the first time he'd had cause to thank his ancestors for the supernatural sense that now had the hairs on the back of his neck standing on end. The way things were going tonight, it wouldn't be the last. The vehicle disappeared around a bend in the foothills, but he had recognized the headlights as belonging to a large vehicle like the SUV that had rammed his Chevy the night before—not that he'd needed confirmation.

"Liz." He gave her a hard shake while reaching for his boots.

"Hmm?"

"There's a car coming. Get up," he ordered.

She bolted upright, narrowly missing the car roof, and swiveled in the direction he stared, but the car was hidden from view amongst the hills. Hawk stuffed his foot into a boot.

Liz looked at him. "What time is it?" Then before he could answer, she asked, "Who would be coming down this road this time of night? Are there homes out here? I don't recall seeing any when I drove out."

"No." He grabbed the second boot. "We've got to get out of here. They'll be here in less than a minute."

She scooted to the end of their makeshift bed and grabbed her boots. After he'd made love to her a second time, he'd insisted they dress. He'd hated not feeling her soft body against his, but the temperature was dropping, and there had been the possibility Reid's men might come back. He hated being right.

Hawk crawled to the door and got out. He scanned the road. The car hadn't come around the nearest bend yet, but they couldn't be more than seconds away.

"Put on that jacket," he ordered and grabbed the rifle and cooler.

"Would Reid's men come back?" she asked.

"It's an SUV," he answered.

Hawk slung the rifle over his shoulder, then, cooler in hand, he slammed the door closed and grasped Liz's hand. The SUV appeared around the last bend.

"Come on." He started them at a run in the direction of the dig.

They neared the decline as the vehicle veered off the road a hundred feet away, headlights dead on them. Hawk pumped his legs faster and nearly flew down the hill. Relief swept through him when Liz kept pace. Headlights cut a path across the desert over their heads. Car doors slammed an instant later.

They reached the farthest cluster of pillars when a voice shouted, "Come on, Professor, you know we saw you."

The Beanstalk.

Hawk pushed Liz behind him and peered around the pillar. Two figures stood on the rise. Jack and his sidekick, The Beanstalk.

"Come on, Professor," The Beanstalk called. "We only want to talk."

Hawk turned and grasped Liz's shoulders. "You moved pretty damn fast. The hills are a hundred and fifty yards. Think you can amp it up a bit?"

She swallowed, but said in a strong voice, "Kick-boxing three days a week and Stairmaster four days a week."

He grinned. "You're in damn good shape. We're going to make for the saddle."

"You don't want anything to happen to your lady friend, do you, Professor?"

Liz's head snapped in the direction of The Beanstalk's voice.

Hawk grasped her jaw and turned her face toward his. "You trust me?" She nodded affirmation and he said, "Good, then do as I say. We're going to run for it, but if they start shooting, I'm going to cover you while you make for the hills." She opened her mouth, but he cut her off. "If you get shot, there's no way I can get you to a doctor." He gave her a smile. "Don't worry. I plan on us making it—together."

She nodded and he released her.

"Professor, you're scaring your lady friend," The Beanstalk called.

Hawk's heart hammered. The Beanstalk had started down the hill. "Grab that cooler and be ready to run," he ordered Liz.

In one fluid motion, Hawk swung the rifle from his shoulder and aimed as he stepped from around the rock.

Then he fired. Both men dropped with shouted curses and began rolling down the hill. Hawk whirled, grabbed Liz's hand, and raced across the open desert.

They were halfway across when a shot rang out.

"Run!" Hawk pushed Liz forward.

He whirled, swung the rifle up, sighted The Beanstalk, and fired again. The big man stumbled as if he'd tripped, then crashed to the ground. Hawk swung the barrel toward Jack and pulled the trigger as he dived for cover. Hawk pivoted and came up short at finding Liz standing twenty feet away.

"God damn it, Liz. Run!"

Hawk reached her in two seconds. He seized her hand and shot forward. She tripped. He yanked her to his side, her feet righted, and they raced forward. Another shot rang out. Dirt kicked up to Liz's right. Red hot fury rammed through him. He hugged Liz closer and dove for the narrow saddle as another shot echoed around them.

They hit the ground, Liz on top of him. Hawk ignored the pain that radiated up his arm and pushed her from him as he rolled onto his stomach and pointed the rifle in the direction of the men. They were running at breakneck speed toward him and Liz. The Beanstalk pointed his pistol.

Hawk sighted The Beanstalk's leg and fired. The Beanstalk dove to the right while Jack dropped.

The Beanstalk rolled and came up on his belly like Hawk, and shouted, "I'll kill you, motherfucker!"

Hawk fired, then pushed to his feet and hauled Liz up with him. "We've got to keep moving."

He pulled her forward, and they broke into a run for the next hill. They rounded the slope as more gunfire sounded. Hawk shoved Liz down and peered around the side. God damn it, the men were nearly halfway to where he and Liz now were. Hawk faced her. His gut wrenched at the stark fear on her face.

"Can you keep going?" he demanded.

She nodded, and they jumped up and started forward. This time, there was no saddle. They had to go over the top of the large rise. How far were Jack and The Beanstalk going to follow them? The two men weren't equipped for getting lost in the mountains.

"Come on," Hawk urged. "We've got to get over that rise before they get around the hill behind us."

Seconds later, they started up the incline. Hawk glanced back. The men weren't in sight. "Think *Stairmaster*," he coaxed through heavy breaths.

Liz was breathing heavier than she had been when they'd started up the hill, but she nodded and picked up speed. Damn, the woman could move. They neared the top, and Hawk looked back in time to see that the men had nearly reached the bottom of the hill behind them. Hawk pulled Liz to the ground. She cried out.

"Crawl," he ordered. She started to look back, but Hawk grabbed her arm. "Keep going."

She crawled forward, and they were over the summit in three seconds. They jumped to their feet and raced to the bottom where Liz came to a halt, breathing hard.

"I need," she drank in more air, "to rest."

"I know. Soon." He pulled her forward.

They moved as fast as they could to the next saddle, where the hills were twice the size they had been when they'd first fled into the foothills.

Shouts went up farther away behind them, and Hawk knew the men were losing ground fast. He and Liz slowed but didn't stop until moonlight dimmed within the deepening shadows of even larger hills.

At last, Hawk brought them to a halt. He listened but heard only silence. "I think we lost them."

A quiet sob broke from Liz.

"Sweetheart." He pulled her into his arms.

"I thought they were going to follow us all night," she cried against his chest.

"They were damned persistent," he agreed.

She began to tremble, and he realized the adrenaline that had kept her going was wearing off. She was going to fall apart. He scanned their surroundings. They'd climbed to an open area against the incline of a gentle rise. He scanned for snakes among the tiny ground shrubs and found none.

"You need to rest." Hawk pried loose the cooler she gripped, then dropped it to the ground and urged her down as he sat beside her. He laid the rifle beside them, and she melted into his arms, tears flowing in earnest.

"It's all right." He stroked her hair.

"I thought they were going to kill you," she sobbed.

Hawk gave a quiet laugh. "That's what had you scared?"

Her head snapped up. "It's not funny."

"I know," he soothed. "You weren't just a little worried they might kill *you*?"

"You were the one they were shooting at."

Hawk remembered the shot that had gone wide to her right. They hadn't been shooting at him that time. "I told you to keep running."

"I wasn't going to leave you to get hurt or captured. They would have killed you."

The determination in her voice didn't surprise him, but the tightening in his chest did. She meant it. She would have put her life on the line for him, just as she had last night when she'd confronted him. It took guts for a woman to stand up to a man his size in a deserted parking lot. And stand up to him she had, even after he'd backed her against the truck. He'd responded to her, despite thinking she'd been sent by Reid. What would he have done if she'd been on the wrong side of this fight?

Hawk startled at the feel of her palm flat against his chest. His heart jumped into high gear as the hand slid upward. Her slender fingers made contact with his neck, and his shaft thickened.

"Liz," he rasped.

She answered by drawing his mouth down to hers. Warm lips met his, and he knew the answer to his question. If she'd been on the wrong side of the fight, he would still be right here with her body pressed close to his. Her tongue slipped past his lips and stroked his. Desire coursed through him like a river of lava. She reached between them and fumbled with his belt.

He broke the kiss. "Liz, if they show up—"

"You said we lost them," she whispered.

"I know, but if I'm wrong—"

He broke off. She'd gone stock still, except for the tremble in her fingers he knew was more from fear than lust. Damn, he was an idiot. She needed him. He glanced in the direction they had come. How long had it been since he'd heard sounds of pursuit, forty-five minutes, an hour? At least that. The men weren't going to find them.

Hawk crushed Liz to him. She pushed at his chest.

"Shh, sweetheart," he soothed. "I need you as much as you need me."

"But you said—"

"I'm an idiot." He pulled her across his lap and covered her mouth with his. His cock pulsed when her rounded ass pressed down on his fast-growing erection. Any minute the damn thing would burst past his button fly and dive straight for her.

She melted in a shuddering mass against him. The kiss turned violent, a slash of sucking lips, tangled tongues, and grazing teeth. Hawk pushed aside the lapel of her blue jean jacket, then fumbled the buttons on the coveralls and palmed her lush breast through the lacy bra. She moaned. He bent his head and sucked the peak through the lace. She clutched his shoulders and arched into his mouth. He sucked harder. She gasped.

He pulled loose the remaining buttons on the coveralls and sank his fingers into the hot moisture of her sex. Liz cried out. Blood roared through his ears, and his cock hardened to the point of agony. She slid a hand up his neck and speared her fingers into his hair. He rammed a finger inside her wet pussy, still sucking her nipple. She tugged hard on his hair.

Need coursed through him with startling heat, but he forced himself to slowly insert a second finger and gently stretch her. She was so damn tight. The thought of ramming his engorged cock inside the small opening sent a dizzying wave of lust through him. He thrust his fingers in and out of her silken passage.

"Hawk," she whimpered.

The need in her voice tightened his chest. He moved to the other breast while fucking her harder with his fingers. She pulsed against the digits. The action bumped her buttocks against his erection. Sweat beaded across his forehead and instantly cooled in the night breeze. Her breath hitched, and he knew she was close to climax. Desire to be inside her clenched body nearly overwhelmed him, but he wasn't done with her yet, not by a long shot.

He released her nipple and buried his face near her ear. "You like this, sweetheart?"

She nodded into his chest.

"Good, because I want to touch you all over…suck you all over."

She shuddered and he felt the tightening of her channel walls around his fingers. He gritted his teeth against the need to shove his cock inside her pussy.

"I don't have a condom with me, Liz. But I'll make you come every way you can imagine, my cock inside your ass while my fingers are inside you."

She ground the cleft of her ass against his cock. His balls tightened. She wanted everything he had to give.

Her walls fluttered, then she spasmed around his fingers. "That's it, baby. Take all you want."

The pulse that beat in her neck thundered against his jaw. He stroked and her legs clamped tight around his hand as another orgasm shook her. Before the shudder had passed, she was reaching for his belt.

Hawk thought he would go out of his mind. She undid the belt and pulled the buttons free. His strangled laugh cut off when she pulled back his boxer briefs and fisted his cock in a tight grip that seared him to the core.

"Liz." He yanked his fingers from inside her.

Her head jerked up. He seized the sleeves of the coveralls and tugged them from her arms. She tumbled from his lap when he dragged the coveralls down her hips. He yanked them free of her legs, then tossed the jacket on the ground beside them and pulled her up to kneel on the fabric. Hawk turned her back to him and undid her bra. The elastic sprang forward, and she tossed it aside, then started to face him.

"Don't move," he ordered. She twisted her head in his direction. He leaned forward and placed a hard kiss on her mouth. "Don't. Move."

She didn't but stared at him from over her shoulder as he

shucked his boots, jeans, underwear, and shirt. When he sidled up behind her on his knees, she froze.

"Remember what I said," he whispered into her hair.

She didn't reply, and he pressed closer, his dick aligned with the crevice of her ass. She sucked in a breath, and Hawk feared he wouldn't be able to keep it together long enough to make good on his promise.

Chapter 9

Liz's stomach was in free fall. She'd never had a man do to her what Hawk promised to do...what he was about to do. He pressed closer. She was acutely aware of his large hands on her hips and the taut control behind the deceptively light grasp. He flattened his palms on the curve of her ass and slid downward.

She drew a sharp breath when his fingers dipped between her soaked folds. Liz held her breath, expecting him to enter her channel again. Instead, he dragged her cream back. She shivered when he gently inserted a lubricated finger into her anus, carefully stretching her. He inserted two fingers, widening the tight ring of muscle in delicious pleasure. By the time he flattened his palms on her ass and gently spread her butt cheeks, she was trembling. He fitted the thick shaft in the crevice and slowly released her buttocks around him.

A thrill raced through her. Hawk pressed his chest against her back, warm and reassuring, then grasped her waist and slowly slid his erection forward through the slickened crevice. Liz leaned into him, and his fingers tightened on her flesh. She reached around and grasped his butt. Muscled flesh tensed beneath her fingers. He thrust upward, then down, then up again. When he moved downward, this time he leaned back, and she felt the bulbous head at the entrance to her anus.

Hawk again opened her wide and this time gently pushed his cock in a fraction. She sucked in a breath, startled by the feel of the tight opening stretched beyond capacity. He'd felt huge while inside her channel, but now he felt mammoth. Liz swallowed, suddenly uncertain, but when his hand slid around her hips and dipped into the moist heat of her slick folds, she melted against him. He pushed his finger deeper as his cock moved a fraction deeper.

He inserted a second finger and gently thrust inside. Liz gasped at the unexpected, pleasurable burn of his cock inching inward. She dug her fingers into his ass and shoved hard to meet the fingers working their wicked magic a second time. Hawk wrapped his free arm around her waist, holding her steady as he pushed into her rectum. She gulped air.

"You all right?" he asked.

She nodded. He gave a low laugh that told her he was well aware of her pleasure, then slowly pulled back until she thought the tip was going to pop out. He thrust in, faster this time, and she flushed when his balls brushed the spot beneath her anus. He began a faster rhythm, his cock in her ass, his fingers keeping pace inside her pussy, and her pulse accelerated. She nestled closer to his groin, angling her hips so that his balls slapped harder.

His arm tightened around her waist, and she realized he understood she wanted all of him. He angled her hips slightly more upward, and his balls hit with more force as he rammed his cock against the outer wall of her womb. She cried out, and his finger began a faster motion inside her slippery channel.

"I never break a promise."

His hoarse words were strained, and she knew he teetered on the edge of orgasm. Feminine pride swelled. Who could make who come first? She rocked harder against his finger, slamming back against his rod as he thrust.

"Liz," he growled.

She kept pace with his rhythm, determined to give as good as she got. His arm clamped iron-like around her waist in a breath-stealing hold. Her channel tightened and clenched around his fingers. A whimper escaped her lips, then she moaned.

"You're not playing fair," he ground out.

Unexpected pressure to her clit sent pleasure spiraling through her. She gasped and seized his arm, as much to keep from losing her balance as in an effort to stop him from bringing her to another hard climax. Wet friction turned hot between her legs. Her clit clenched, and an orgasm fractured through her. She cried out. He pistoned into her, the rhythm so hard and fast that the spasm took her breath. Liz cried out his name. He growled and thickened inside her ass.

Then exploded.

Hawk didn't want to travel any more tonight if he could help it. Hell, he didn't want to move from on top of Liz. But he slid from her nonetheless, pulling her close. Their sweat-slicked bodies would cool off all too quickly in the tiny breeze, but he was going to hold her naked body for a final few moments before he insisted they get dressed. He detected a tremble in her, but knew it wasn't from the cool night air. Chances were the gravity of what they'd just done was crashing in on her…or what she *thought* of what they'd just done, to be more accurate.

"I don't regret a thing," he whispered. Except getting her into this mess to begin with. But he'd deal with Reid tomorrow.

"We're in an unusual situation," she replied.

Hawk jerked from his thoughts. "What?"

"The circumstances are tense. I'm scared—"

"Yeah, but you sure as hell weren't scared this afternoon when you showed up at the dig or earlier, when we were in the Land Cruiser."

She muttered something into his chest.

"What?" he demanded.

"Young whippersnapper."

He laughed, then rolled on top of her again. "Could a *young whippersnapper* do all the things I just did to you?" He couldn't discern a blush but knew by the way her lashes dropped that she was flaming. "Look at me, Liz."

She hesitated, then shifted her eyes back to his face.

"You're beautiful and smart, and you've got guts."

"I'll take that," she replied, and he laughed again.

He stared at her for a long moment, seriously considering making love to her a second time, when she said, "They've amped things up, haven't they?"

He released a breath and shifted back to her side. "I should have known last night when they pulled that stunt in the parking lot, but I still figured that they were trying to scare me."

"You acted like they really were going to mow me down with that SUV," she said.

That's what he'd thought at the time, but then the light of day had him thinking even Reid wasn't that stupid. Hawk nodded.

"Last night, they saw you risk your life for me, and you knew what they would think. That's why they slashed my tires. They were telling you they would hurt me if you didn't comply." Liz traced a finger along his jaw. "I'm so sorry."

He grasped her hand and pressed a kiss to her fingers. "You didn't do anything wrong."

"No, but, like you said, I have lousy timing." She released a breath. "But if they intended to use me against you, why the direct attack tonight?" Before he could answer, she added, "Because something happened after they sabotaged the cars."

"I said you were smart. Let's get dressed." Hawk pulled her into a sitting position and scanned the ground for her bra and panties. They lay a few feet to the right. He scooped them up and handed them to her. "This is as good a place as any to catch some sleep. I want to head back by first light."

"First light?" she burst out.

"It's not safe tonight. They're sure to have someone watching the cars." He put on his boxer briefs.

"Shouldn't we try to get to the road?" she asked.

"We're fifteen miles off Highway 87, as the crow flies. Travelling all night through these hills isn't a great idea."

"Staying here is?"

He grabbed his jeans. "It's our best choice."

Liz examined her panties and turned them around before sticking one foot then the other into the legs. "You don't think there's a chance they're still looking for us?"

"They're not the type to rough it in the mountains." Hawk paused in pulling on his jeans to watch her shimmy her lace panties over her hips.

"Damn it, Liz. Do that a second time, and I'll take off those panties and kiss you all over."

Her head snapped up.

"Don't doubt I can do it," he said.

"We just finished," she said in an incredulous voice.

"That wouldn't stop me."

She hesitated, and he realized she was considering testing him. He waited, wondering how long it would take her to decide. When she reached for the bra, he figured embarrassment had won out. That was all right. He wouldn't wait too long to prove he didn't make idle statements. He grabbed his shirt and, a minute later, they were dressed.

Hawk picked up the jacket, then settled against the incline of the hill alongside the rifle and cooler and extended a hand. "Come here."

She took two steps and lowered herself beside him. He pulled her against his chest, then laid the jacket over her shoulders.

"We can't be sure they won't still be watching the cars early morning. I don't want another run-in with The Beanstalk," he said.

"The Beanstalk." She grinned against his chest. "You mentioned him last night in the parking lot. Why do you call him that?"

"Did you get a look at the guy? He's tall and skinny."

"But dangerous," she murmured.

Yeah. More dangerous than he'd realized.

Chapter 10

The following morning at dawn, Liz stopped walking and jerked her gaze to Hawk, who already had the rifle pointed in the direction of the sound to their right. Sunlight seeped across the early morning sky, casting enough light into the wide saddle they were crossing to make them easy targets. A murmur of voices floated to them from around the hill.

Hawk motioned her to go to the left toward the hillside. She quietly followed his lead as he sidestepped in that direction. Her heart pounded. There were no trees or rocks to use as cover. If Hawk shot one of the men, would the other shoot him before he could shoot back? They were so close to the dig—fifteen minutes, Hawk had estimated. Reid must be desperate to have sent his men into the mountains after them again.

A man appeared around the bend. "Whoa!" he called, his eyes glued to Hawk's rifle.

He lifted his hands to show he held no weapon, but Liz saw the revolver strapped to his waist. She gave a small cry at recognizing the grey uniform of law enforcement and the mounted unit patch on his arm.

Hawk lowered the rifle. "You almost got yourself shot."

"I see that." The man glanced from him to Liz. "Professor Hawkins? Ms. Williams?"

Hawk nodded.

"You two all right?" he asked.

"Yes," Hawk replied.

The man pulled the radio from his belt. "Joe, I found them fifteen minutes to the north. They're alive and well. We'll meet you back at the cars."

The radio clicked, then, "Roger that," Joe replied over the radio. "Over."

Liz startled at the feel of Hawk's hand on her shoulder and leaned into him as he pulled her close.

The man clipped the radio back to his belt. "You've got some worried friends and relatives."

"Who alerted you?" Hawk asked.

"Ms. Williams' daughter reported her missing. We would have had no idea to look for her out here, but the sergeant who questioned her remembered a call from a Ms. Gloria Alameda who said you didn't come home last night, Professor Hawkins."

Hawk shook his head. "That's the first time I'm thankful for nosy neighbors."

The officer nodded. "When Ms. Williams' daughter mentioned your name, he put two and two together." He gave them a penetrating look. "The officer who drove out here found your two vehicles and realized something was wrong. What happened out here last night?"

"We had a couple of men shooting at us," Hawk said.

The officer's gaze sharpened. "You know who they were?"

"I do," Hawk replied. "We can give a full statement."

He nodded. "Let's get back." He looked at Liz. "Your daughter is very worried."

DETECTIVES LYONS LOOKED AT HAWK FROM ACROSS THE SMALL table in the interview room. The police had separated him and Liz when they'd arrived at the precinct an hour ago.

"You're absolutely positive the men were Harry Jones and Jack Phillips?" Lyons asked.

"I've seen them half a dozen times," Hawk said. "The Beanstalk—Harry Jones—drives that SUV that tried to run us down the other night."

"You recognized him that night?"

Hawk shook his head.

"What about a license plate number?" the detective asked.

"I didn't have time to take notes. You have a witness who saw the whole thing. Didn't they get it?"

Lyons' leaned back in his chair. "Ms. Williams told you we had a witness?"

Hawk nodded. "Yes."

"Then you know that witness saw you get rough with her."

Hawk had wondered when the detective would get around to what happened between him and Liz. The detective's attitude had been subtle but aggressive. "We had a disagreement. I thought Reid sent her."

"You think it's okay to get rough with the women Mr. Reid sends your way?"

"No," Hawk answered honestly. Saying more would only play into the detective's hands.

Lyons stared for a long moment, then glanced down at

the small notebook sitting on the table in front of him. "You were carrying a falling-block rifle when the rangers found you." Lyons looked up at Hawk. "Do you carry a rifle with you everywhere you go?"

"The rifle stays in my truck. When Liz and I found her slashed tires and my cut brake line, I kept it close. Good thing I did."

"Yeah?" Lyons said.

Hawk kept his gaze locked with his. "Yeah. Reid's thugs came back—and shot at us."

The door opened and another detective entered with a woman. "Professor Hawkins, I'm Detective Marlow, and this is Assistant DA Brenda O'Malley."

Hawk stood and shook hands with them.

"We've been trying to find solid evidence against Vance Reid for five years," Brenda said. "Could you identify the men who shot at you in a line-up?"

"Yes," Hawk said.

"Good. Come on."

Lyons stood, and Hawk followed the three of them from the room. They reached a small room with a one way glass. Liz was there with a female detective. She gave him a tremulous smile. He crossed to her, and she nearly fell into his arms.

Hawk hugged her tight for a moment, then pulled back. "You ready for this?"

She nodded. "It's gotta be done."

"Okay," Hawk told Brenda.

The men were filed out, and Hawk and Liz each picked out their two attackers. He saw the fear that flickered in Liz's eyes before she was able to hide it, and he knew what he had to do.

"This is ridiculous." Liz looked from Emma to Hawk. They sat across from her at the kitchen table that evening.

"You're the one being ridiculous," Emma said. "Professor Hawkins is right. You can't stay here alone tonight."

"Emma," Liz began, but Hawk cut her off.

"Liz, if you're not going to think of yourself, think of Emma. What happens if Reid sends someone to your place while she's here?"

That stopped Liz cold. "Em, you have to go away until this is over."

"What? No way." Emma shook her head. "You're staying. I'm staying."

"This isn't a game." Liz looked at Hawk. "I'm right. You know it. Tell her."

"Maybe," he said.

"No way," Emma exploded.

"Hold on," Hawk said before Emma could go ballistic. "Let's start with tonight, shall we?" He looked at Liz. "We've had a rough day. How about we hunker down for the night, the three of us, get some rest, then see what the police come up with tomorrow?"

Liz hesitated.

"I'm not going anywhere," Em said.

"You will if I say so," Liz replied. "But I'll agree to tonight. Then," she looked at her daughter, "tomorrow, you will do exactly what I say."

Emma's mouth tightened. "Maybe."

Liz was too exhausted to argue.

Emma rose from the table. "I'm going downstairs to my place and get some studying done."

Liz nodded. "I'll call you for dinner."

"Three's a crowd, Mom."

"You're coming for dinner, or I'm coming for you," Liz said. "I'd say about an hour."

Her daughter nodded and left.

Liz released a breath. "Will she be all right downstairs?"

"Is there a separate entrance to her basement apartment?" Hawk asked.

Liz shook her head. "No. She has to enter inside through the hallway."

"Then she'll be all right. No one will get past me to her."

Or you, Liz knew he was thinking.

"How does steak sound?" she asked.

"Barbecue?" he asked.

"I could fire up the gas grill."

He rose. "Leave it to me."

She stood, and he grasped her hand. A tremor rippled through her when his fingers tightened gently around hers and drew her close. He surprised her by placing a kiss on her forehead.

"Come on." He led her from the kitchen and started down the hallway.

"Hawk—"

"Which room is yours?" he asked.

"Emma's here," she said.

He opened the first door on the right to the bathroom, then closed it.

"Hawk," Liz said.

He opened the second door to the left, which was her office.

He looked at her. "Very nice." He closed the door and stepped to the door on the left.

Her heart was pounding. "If Emma comes up here, she'll hear us," Liz protested as he opened the door to her room.

Hawk stepped inside and led her to the queen sized bed.

He grasped her shoulders, bent, and brushed his lips against hers. Liz stilled, unable to deny she was glad for the warmth of his mouth against hers and the pressure of his fingers in the flesh of her shoulders. She suddenly realized she wanted him, needed him. Before she could respond, he pulled away and drew back the covers. When he eased her onto the bed, her heart thumped even harder.

He tugged the covers up over her and sat on the edge of the bed. "You need some rest.

"Rest?" she repeated.

"Rest." He smiled. "You expected something else?"

She flushed.

His brows rose. "Maybe you were hoping for something else?"

"Emma's here," Liz said in a whisper.

He nodded, and she couldn't tear her eyes from his face.

"Later." He kissed her forehead again, then left.

She stared at the closed door, uncertain she could let him walk away so easily. Then she closed her eyes.

***

"You tell GFW they can make payment on time or talk to our lawyers." Liz spoke into the phone at her home office to Ben Dixon, CFO of GFW, Leland Industries' largest buyer the following morning. "You received the product, Ben. We expect the final payment in five days—per our contract."

She shifted and winced when butt muscles screamed. She'd slept through dinner and clear through the night, which probably hadn't helped. A tremor radiated through her stomach. Was it the run or the hard *workout* Hawk had given her that had her body sore?

"Liz." Ben's voice dragged her back to the present. "We've done business too long for there to be this kind of animosity."

"And we've done business long enough for me to know when I'm being stonewalled," she replied. "I read the *Wall Street Journal*. Leland Industries isn't about to finance GFW's merger with Suyama Industries."

"One month, Liz. That's all I'm asking," he pleaded.

Her assistant Karen walked in and pointed to her watch. Liz nodded. She had a conference call with a new start-up design company in five minutes.

"Tell you what," she said into the phone, "you give Leland Industries the interest you'll make on keeping our money in *your* bank, and you've got a deal."

Silence.

"Kind of defeats the purpose, doesn't it?" she asked.

"Liz—"

"No," she cut in. "You're asking us to lose money so that you can make money. We won't do it, Ben."

He sighed. "I'll talk to Anderson. Maybe he can offer some sort of incentive."

"Five days," she repeated.

"You sure you won't come over to the dark side and work for us?" he asked.

She laughed. "You make this offer every time you get tired of arguing with me."

"Hell, yeah," he agreed. "But I mean it."

He'd meant it every time he said it over the last ten years. Ben wasn't a bad guy, but today was a perfect example of how GFW did business, and she didn't like it.

"I'll talk to you later, Ben."

"Think about it," he said. "Seriously."

"I have. Now you talk to your boss." She hung up.

Karen sat down in the chair across from Liz's desk. "Are they going to pay?"

Liz leaned back in her chair. "Hard to say. The interest they'll make by withholding payment is enough to induce even good old honest Abe Lincoln to give thought to holding out. What have you got?" She nodded toward the pink slips of paper in Karen's hand while reaching for the quarterly production report she'd been poring over when Ben called.

"Two messages from Suzy Chang and one from Professor Hawkins," Karen replied.

Liz's head jerked up before she could halt the action.

Karen's brows rose. "That must have been some night in the mountains."

Liz's heart raced. Why would he be calling when she was meeting him and Emma in two hours at the university? She blew out a breath she hoped said *last night was an experience I don't care to repeat,* and said, "A person doesn't get shot at every day."

"No. And they don't get stuck in the mountains with a man like Professor Hawkins every day, either. I saw his picture in the paper." Karen waggled her eyebrows. "The man is drop-dead gorgeous."

"It was life or death, Karen. Gorgeous had nothing to do with it. Not to mention the man's twelve years younger than me."

Karen's gaze sharpened, and Liz realized her mistake when her assistant said, "You noticed that, did you?"

Liz shrugged. "It would be hard not to notice a man like him." When in doubt, fall back on the truth. "But that doesn't change the fact we were running for our lives."

Karen's expression sobered. "Hard to believe all this is over some land."

"Land that's worth enough money to make our dispute with GFW look like couch change."

At least Hawk's goal had been accomplished. Artifacts supporting his theories that the site was Paleo-Indian had been discovered on the north-east section of the land, butting up to and reaching into Reid's land, which explained Reid's desperation to get to Hawk. Liz glanced at the clock. Six-thirty. Injunctions would already have been filed to stop all building until experts were brought in to assess the find. Hawk would be one of those experts.

"I still can't believe the police can't arrest the guys who shot at you," Karen said.

Liz had been just as surprised. But Hawk had known the police wouldn't be able to connect Reid to the two men they identified—a fact that wasn't going to stop Hawk from dealing with Reid, despite Liz's attempts to dissuade him. According to him, the only good thing that had come out of their attack was the fact that, since the case was now high profile, Harry Jones—also known as The Beanstalk—and his partner Jack Phillips wouldn't be able to get near Liz again.

That didn't mean someone else wouldn't try, which was why an unmarked police car sat outside and why Liz had agreed to work from home today. That and Hawk's threat to follow her to the plant and stick by her side all day if she didn't stay home. The question in Em's eyes when Liz had explained what happened had been bad enough. She didn't want to confirm her daughter's suspicions by having her professor follow her mother around all day. Liz had to admit, working from home in jeans and a T-shirt was a welcome respite from dressing for work. She needed the break after the last couple days.

"You've got that call," Karen said.

Liz nodded. "You go ahead and take off."

"You sure?"

Liz nodded. "Yep."

"Same place, same time tomorrow," Karen asked.

Liz laughed. "Yeah. I think Emma would have a fit if I left the house just yet." But it wasn't Emma she was worried about.

Half an hour later, Liz flipped off the bedroom light and stepped into the hallway. A hulking figure stood at the far end, silhouetted against the soft light behind him in the foyer. Not The Beanstalk but a stranger inside her house. She whirled back into the room, slamming the door shut.

Liz turned the tiny lock then raced to the window on the far wall. She wound the handle and the window began to roll outward. A crash against the door caused her to jump. Her heart thudded. Where were the police? The door banged with the man's weight against the wood. Liz fought panic. He'd be inside and upon her before she could open the window and climb outside. She released the window handle, grabbed the cordless from the nightstand, and jabbed nine-one-one.

One ring, then a voice said, "Nine-one-one, what is your emergency?"

"Someone—" The door creaked again and splintered.

Liz dropped the phone and grabbed the crystal lamp on the nightstand. She ripped the shade from the lamp and raced to the wall beside the door. Hands shaking, she raised the lamp as the door gave way beneath the gorilla's weight.

He propelled two steps into the room, and she swung the lamp with all her strength. The thick crystal slammed into the side of his neck with a sickening crack. She swung the lamp again. His arm shot up, and he wrenched it from her grip. Iron fingers seized her wrist, and the back of his hand made hard contact against her cheek.

Her head jerked sideways, and pain shot through her cheek. He dragged her forward. She stumbled. The goon yanked her upright as they crossed from the bedroom into the hallway. Spots raced across her vision. Liz fought nausea and kicked his leg.

"Fucking bitch," he cursed.

She drew breath for a scream, but he clamped a large hand over her mouth and jerked her against him. Hot breath covered her ear. She forced back the whimper that rose to her lips.

"Keep your fucking mouth shut." His voice, low and deep, resonated in her ear.

Where were the police that were supposed to be outside? Emma and Hawk weren't expecting her at the university for another hour and a half. She fought tears.

Keep it together. If Reid intended to kill you, you'd be dead.

He needed her as leverage against Hawk.

They reached the foyer, and the man turned left into the family room, instead of right toward the front door as expected. He was headed for the garage beyond the kitchen, which was part of the large area that made up the family room.

Liz caught sight of the knife block sitting on the counter beside the door that opened into the garage. Her stomach knotted. Could she stab another human being? Once Reid threatened to kill her, Hawk would give into Reid's demands, then Reid would kill her and Hawk.

A vision rose of Hawk stepping from the door to the university parking lot on a deserted night, and a bullet ripping through his massive chest. No one would be there to stop the gush of blood as he crashed to the asphalt, then bled to death.

They reached the door.

"Keep your mouth shut, or I'll come back for your daughter," her attacker ordered.

Liz froze.

Emma.

He released her mouth and opened the door. As he crossed the threshold, Liz closed her fingers around the handle of the nine-inch chef's knife. The blade slid noiselessly from its wooden sheath. Her heart hammered. They stepped into the garage, and he started around the front of the Land Cruiser. She rammed the knife into his thigh. Her stomach roiled at the feel of the blade slicing into his muscle.

He bellowed an animal's cry, twisting in a frenzied movement. His grip on her loosened. She yanked the knife free and forced back bile when slick, warm blood covered her hand. She stabbed again and pushed free. He crashed to his knees in front of the Toyota, clutching his leg where the hilt protruded like an all-too-lifelike Halloween prank. Liz reached back, steadying herself on the fender as she sidled around the car. Blood spread in a dark stain across the thug's thousand-dollar suit's trouser leg.

He grabbed the knife, and his face contorted as he yanked it free. He threw it aside. The knife clattered on the cement and skittered under the Land Cruiser. He lifted his head, and wild eyes met hers. She retreated another step, then froze. He was nearly as close to the door as she was. A grotesque smile twisted his mouth. He'd realized the same thing.

Liz lunged forward, slapped the garage door opener, and whirled. The mechanical door jerked into motion and the man's heavy grunt told her he'd shoved to his feet. She pulled down paint cans, cleaning bottles and anything else she could grab from the shelf on her right. Debris bounced off the Land Cruiser and clattered to the floor. A crash sounded behind her, and the man bellowed in pain. The door had lifted a mere foot from the ground. Liz dropped to her belly to roll underneath.

A large hand seized her leg. She twisted onto her back. He was on his knees, blood gushing from his leg as he grabbed for her other leg with his free hand. She kicked his face. Bone and cartilage cracked beneath the ball of her foot. Blood spurted from his nose, but he held tight, while grabbing for her other leg. She kicked again and pulled loose.

Liz rolled under the garage door, onto her feet, and hit a solid wall. Steel arms banded around her. She blinked against the glare of the streetlight behind them and raked nails across her new attacker's face.

He grunted. "Liz."

Tears streamed down her face. "Let me go, you son of a bitch."

"Mom!"

Liz grimaced against the fog of fear that clouded her brain. A large hand seized the hand with blood on it. A noise behind her caused her to jerk her head around, and she saw her attacker stumble from the garage. An animal growl emanated from the man holding her. She startled at the sight of Emma at his side. A siren wailed in the distance.

The man holding her stepped around her, and Liz sucked in a breath.

Hawk.

Chapter 11

Lava-hot fury rammed through Hawk. The man who emerged from the garage had tried to kill Liz. Her attacker veered right, heading for the neighbor's yard. Hawk dove for him. They crashed to the concrete. Hawk reared up and drove a fist into his already bloody face.

"Hawk!" Liz shouted.

"Professor Hawkins!" Emma cried.

Hawk jumped to his feet, dragging the man up with him. "I warned Reid," Hawk growled.

Hawk slammed a fist into his stomach. The man doubled over with a heavy grunt. Hawk swung an uppercut to his jaw. The man flew back and landed on the neighbor's lawn. Hawk leapt onto him like a wild animal, fist raised. Weight dragged his right arm down as he threw the punch, and Liz jerked forward from the force of gripping his arm. She fell on top of the man. Hawk seized her arm and pulled her off him.

"Hawk!" she shouted as he raised another fist, aiming for the man.

She grabbed his arm again. He yanked his gaze onto her.

"I'm okay," she said.

He blinked.

"He wasn't trying to kill me."

"What?"

"The blood," she said. "It's his, not mine."

Hawk glanced from her blood-stained pants to the man. Blood soaked his face where his nose had been broken, and his left trouser leg was drenched with blood. The guy moaned.

Gentle fingers cupped Hawk's jaw, and Liz turned his face toward hers. "I'd rather you didn't go to jail for killing him," she said.

Hawk shoved away from Reid's man, pulling Liz into his arms as he gained his feet. He held her, unable to do anything else. He became aware of the blare of an approaching police siren and registered the fact that Emma stood a few feet away.

"Damn it," he cursed. "Emma...."

Liz turned and opened her arms. Emma launched herself into her mother's embrace, tears streaming down her face. Hawk looked up to find neighbors up and down the street standing on their lawns and on the sidewalk, watching. Blue and red lights bounced off the houses an instant before a cruiser sped around the corner. Hawk started toward the curb as the car came to a skidding halt in front of Liz's house. The driver's side door swung open, and a cop jumped out, hand resting on his gun.

"We're all right, officer," Hawk said.

The cop's eyes flicked to the man lying on the grass as he took two steps to meet Hawk. "What happened?"

The other cop came around the hood.

Hawk pointed to Liz's attacker. "That man broke into Ms. Williams' home and attacked her."

The police officer's gaze shifted to his partner. "Check him out."

The other cop started around Hawk.

"What do you have to do with this?" the officer Hawk was talking to asked.

"Ms. Williams' daughter and I happened to pull up when she was running from the garage."

The cop flicked another glance at Liz's attacker, then looked back at Hawk. "Looks like she didn't need any help."

Hawk nodded.

Liz and Emma appeared at his side, Liz's arm around Emma.

"You all right, ma'am?" the officer asked.

"It's not my blood," she said, then blurted, "The police."

"Yes, ma'am," the officer replied.

She shook her head and looked at Hawk. "The plain-clothes officers."

"What is she talking about?" the officer demanded.

"We're part of an investigation against Vance Reid," Hawk said. "She was supposed to have police protection to stop this from happening." Hawk looked at her. "Where was the car, Liz?"

"It's the white Chevy across the street."

Hawk and the cop turned. Hawk started toward the empty vehicle, but the cop stopped him. "Stay here."

Hawk slipped an arm around Liz as the three of them watched the cop cross to the Chevy. He stopped on the driver's side, then turned and murmured something into the radio clipped to his shoulder. When he leaned into the window, Hawk knew the cops were there, but not conscious. He hoped like hell they weren't dead.

His blood went cold. How was he going to protect Liz until Reid was behind bars?

Two hours later, Liz stared at Hawk. Unlike Emma, who sat beside her at the kitchen table, Hawk stood, staring down at her with a fierce determination that made him look very much like a hawk about to swoop down on its prey. And she was the prey.

She shook her head. "I've said it a dozen times, I'll say it again. You're out of your mind." He opened his mouth to reply, but she cut him off. "It's late. We're all tired."

They had learned that the two plainclothes officers who'd been stationed outside her house had been drugged, the coffee given to them by a little old lady who'd claimed to live down the block. After the police finished questioning them, Hawk had returned with Liz and Emma to their place. And now refused to leave.

"You'll think differently of this in the morning," Liz said.

"It's my fault you're in this mess to begin with," he said.

She softened. "That's ridiculous. You had no control over the fact that Reid's men showed up when you and I were talking at the university. You couldn't know a simple conversation would turn into this."

"Simple conversation?" Emma snorted.

Liz shot her a quelling look.

"I've only just found you, Liz. I have no intention of losing you," Hawk said.

Liz jerked her gaze to him. "Hawk," she began, then remembered her daughter. "Mr. Reid is in custody. He can't hurt me."

Hawk locked gazes with her. "He's out on bail."

Fear clenched her stomach. "You can't know that."

"That phone call a few minutes ago was from a friend. I know."

"They only arrested him a few hours ago," she whispered.

"Damn it, Liz. I see the fear in your eyes. You can't expect me to walk away."

She scowled. "I'm not asking you to walk away. You just can't live in this house."

"It's not permanent," Emma said.

"It'll be months before his case goes to trial," Liz said.

"Mom—"

"Enough, Emma," Liz cut in. "We need to get some sleep."

"You're right," Em agreed. "It's very late, and I have class tomorrow." She rose and leaned toward Hawk. "*Talk* to her."

"Emma!" Liz warned.

"I'm going to say goodnight to Professor Hawkins' friends, then go to bed," Emma said.

By *friends*, Emma meant Elan Blackbear, the youngest of the four men Hawk had guarding the house. Hawk wasn't taking any chances.

"With that army outside, you can go home and get some rest," Liz told him.

Emma paused in the arched doorway to the foyer. "You forgot something, Mom."

Liz's heart skipped a beat. What was wrong now?

Emma smiled. "Who's going to protect you from yourself?" She turned and disappeared into the foyer.

A moment later, the front door opened, and Emma said, "Hey," then the door clicked shut.

"I think you played matchmaker bringing that boy here," Liz said.

"He was a good choice," Hawk said. "And he's no boy."

Hawk grasped her arm and pulled her to her feet.

He slid his arm around her. "Neither am I."

She lifted her head and looked into his eyes. The determination remained, but a soft light tempered the hard edge.

Butterflies skimmed the inside of her stomach. In the two days she'd known him, he'd risked his life as many times for her. He lowered his mouth toward hers.

Was she going to let a few years stop her from getting to know this man? Hawk's lips covered hers, slow, easy...with an intent that told her a long night lay ahead of them and she would be sore all over again. Was she going to let him get away?

Liz sighed into the kiss, then wrapped her arms around his neck.

No way.

Sneak Peek of Abducted

Tarah Scott and Evan Trevane

Blurb for Abducted

He's too hot, too smart, too young... and too damn hard to resist.

The El Paso fashion gala was slated to be the hottest event of the year and a must do if Liz Monahan, the creative brains behind Nina Bruno Designs, was to vault the company to the big time. Circumstances put Liz at the party in one of her own creations, escorted by a young, handsome model hired to show her off to the well-known and well-established. But Liz didn't count on her date being an undercover Texas Ranger who is investigating a human trafficking ring. She also didn't count on being kidnapped and trafficked herself.

When Texas Ranger Ben Hunter slips away from Liz Monahan at the gala and begins his investigation, he couldn't be more surprised to arrive in Juarez, Mexico to find her held captive by infamous human trafficker Carlos Sanchez. In order to save her, Ben must commit murder. Hers.

Chapter 1

Nina Bruno Designs caters to the modern woman. The mature woman who knows that life begins after forty.

Liz mentally repeated the litany as she blinked at the strobe of photoflashes illuminating the night outside the limousine. The car slowed behind a line of other limos entering a circular drive and Francis Remmey's estate came into full view. Spotlights crisscrossed the Edwardian columns and stone façade of the mansion.

Only a few hours ago, she had been giddy at the prospect of getting caught on camera by the reporters that now crowded each approaching vehicle and lined both sides of the walkway leading to the hacienda's steps. It seemed the entire state of Texas had converged on El Paso for the fashion event of the year, the fifth annual *G International Gala* hosted by Larissa Remmey, owner of *G International* fashion magazine.

Now, however, getting noticed was a double-edged sword.

Liz shifted her attention to the two co-workers sitting across from her. Richard Anderson, VP of Marketing of Nina Bruno Designs, and Brenda Pierce, Head Designer.

"This is a bad idea," Liz said.

"You and your dress are going to be a hit," Richard said. "Stop worrying."

The knot in her stomach cinched tighter. "What in God's name were we thinking? We have an arsenal of models, any of whom would pant at the opportunity to debut the first design in our winter collection. Just because Lisa wasn't able to accept our offer to replace Tanya didn't mean we couldn't find someone else. Why didn't we try?"

"Name someone else who lives in El Paso," Richard said. "Even better, name someone old enough who would fit into that dress. You're the one who's been selling the idea that older women don't want to see teenagers modeling the clothes they buy."

Liz tugged the bustier top higher. She had to remember to make the darts deeper for women her size. "My *attributes* aren't enough to warrant me modeling this dress."

"Yes, they are," he replied. "But the point is moot. We had no choice."

Liz tamped down on the panic that began three hours ago upon watching the news report that their New York buyer Genevra had declared bankruptcy. That meant the three hundred thousand dollar payment they were expecting in sixty days wasn't coming. An hour after they'd learned about Genevra, they got a call from a local reporter that the model they'd hired to debut their winter-line dress had just been seen getting into a limo outside her downtown El Paso hotel wearing a layered chiffon flamenco-style dress that screamed Jorge Estonia—their direct competition in Dallas.

In a span of three hours, Nina Bruno Designs—the company she had poured her life savings into—had gone from the verge of financial independence to teetering on financial ruin. The worst part was that the employees and investors now expected her to pull off what Tanya could have accomplished in her sleep.

When Brenda had approached Liz with the design early that spring, she'd fallen in love with the strapless, bustier-style leather bodice and chic gathered skirt design. But the thought never entered her mind that she might be forced to wear the twenty-seven inch dress in an effort to keep the company from going under.

Another Xenon-flash flared, jarring her from her thoughts.

Brenda leaned forward and straightened the strap on Liz's three-inch heel sandal. "You look as good as Tanya in that dress."

Liz pursed her lips. "We promoted Tanya as the model for this dress. People are expecting her, not a replacement ten years older, and certainly not a company executive."

"You're only seven years older," Richard said. "But you don't look a day over her thirty-seven."

Liz shot him a dry look. "If that's meant to boost my ego, it doesn't."

Richard returned the look. "Get your priorities straight, Liz. You want our first invitation to Larissa's gala to be our last? Without this event, our winter collection ends up in bargain stores and we don't get invited to another major fashion show this year."

Liz knew he really meant, 'We won't be in a position to go to another major fashion show this year—maybe no other fashion show ever.' The company no longer had the luxury of growing slowly. This was Nina Bruno Designs' only chance to stay in business.

"Damn that bitch," he muttered.

"Richard," Liz admonished.

He shook his head. "Don't start with me. You hired Tanya."

"She's the best model in her age bracket," Liz said. "And, as you pointed out, one of the few who would fit into this dress."

His eyes lowered to her chest. "Not anymore."

From the corner of his eye, Ben saw another limo stop in front of the estate and turned his head in time to see the rear door open and Richard Anderson emerge from the vehicle. Anderson turned and extended a hand into the car's open doorway. A slim arm reached toward him and cameras flashed in quick succession as a long, shapely leg stretched toward the paving stones. Elizabeth Monahan's face came into view, illuminated by camera lights.

Ben lifted an eyebrow in appreciation as she rose to her full five foot nine—no, he dropped his attention to her three-inch heels—her six-foot *height*. He raised his gaze up those long legs, then the pleated skirt that brushed toned thighs, and blew out a silent whistle. *Whoa.* Her breasts nearly spilled over the bodice of the leather top—the dress that was kicking off the winter collection for Nina Bruno. His appreciative mood vanished. What was the Creative Director of Nina Bruno Designs doing wearing the dress Tanya Xavier—his date—was supposed to be modeling?

NB Designs had hired him as Tanya's escort. He was the arm candy that said, *Buy this dress and land a man like me.*

Something had gone wrong for Elizabeth Monahan to be wearing the main attraction. Was he to escort her or did the change of plans include another escort? Maybe she decided that Tanya would wear another dress. He didn't like surprises. She should have called. But why would she? He was just the hired help.

Richard Anderson slipped Ms. Monahan's hand into the crook of his arm and led her toward the steps. Toward Ben. She glanced left, and the press snapped photos and thrust microphones toward her. Then she spotted him. Her brow furrowed. Understanding hardened her expression and Ben read in her eyes a mirror image of his thoughts: *What the hell are you doing here?* He'd bet a thousand bucks someone forgot to call him to cancel. Damn good thing, too, because he'd have come no matter what.

They reached him.

"This isn't going to work," Elizabeth hissed under her breath.

She had that right. Was that a hint of nipple peeking over the bodice of her dress? The damn thing was scandalous, even for these over-the-top designers.

"You knew Adam was going to be here, Liz," Richard said in a low voice. "You hired him."

Adam Billings. His alias.

She flashed a dazzling smile that caught Ben off guard before he caught sight of a reporter pointing a camera at them. The camera flashed and her smile didn't falter when she said under her breath to Anderson, "You know good-and-well I forgot he was going to be here, and you conveniently forgot to remind me."

She darted a glance over her shoulder, clearly worried her whispered words might have been overheard by a reporter who had edged closer. Not much chance of that happening amid the babble of other reporters.

She really couldn't ask him to leave, but he had to play the part of a pliant employee. Ben angled his head away from the reporters in case any of the vultures could read lips. "I can leave, if you prefer, ma'am."

"Liz, half of Texas is watching us," Anderson said. "Make a scene now, and it'll be all over the state before the evening is over. We need him."

Something Ben couldn't quite define flickered in her gaze, then she shot Anderson a look to kill. "I sleep with the CEO, Richard. You're fired."

Ben bit back a laugh.

Anderson nodded. "Sure thing, Liz. As soon as the party's over, I'll pack up my desk." He transferred her hand to Ben's arm. "She's all yours. Good luck."

The determination to get to know her better had formed two days ago, during a photo shoot with him and Tanya after the Thompson Agency sent him in to replace the model originally hired to escort Tanya.

Ben glanced at her legs, then reminded himself not to combine business with pleasure. So what if he hadn't expected to see her tonight dressed in an outfit that heated his blood? He had to get inside the Remmey's mansion. Business now. Pleasure later.

Liz gripped his arm and he had the feeling she was considering a quick getaway. Ben covered her hand with his —if nothing else to keep her from bolting. Liz Monahan was his ticket through the door.

He led her up the stairs and a man dressed like a British soldier opened the door at their approach. They entered the foyer and the door closed behind them, cutting off the voices. Ben squinted against a glow of chandelier light bouncing off the white marble floor. A sweeping staircase to their right led to a gallery that encircled the foyer. Directly ahead, three arched doorways opened to the rear of the estate. An escape route if anything went wrong. But Liz Monahan as his date might ensure nothing went wrong. Slipping away from her would be easier than ditching Tanya. If Liz was all business as she had been during their shoot two days ago, she wouldn't miss him.

He steered her left, toward the music wafting through an arched doorway. They reached the room and he turned Liz right in the direction of a dancefloor near a twelve-piece orchestra.

Ben waited until they'd passed a man and woman talking in low tones before whispering to her, "Is that true?"

She looked up. "What?"

He leaned closer. "Do you really sleep with the CEO?"

Frustration flickered across her features. "No, but I'd give him a go if he really would fire Richard."

Ben laughed. He just bet she would. "He's right, you know. You are the one who hired me."

Her eyes narrowed. "*You* I *can* fire—and don't think your good looks will stop me."

So she had noticed. During the photo shoot she'd appraised him like a prize horse.

Ben shrugged. "I'm an independent contractor, if you recall. I don't have to work for Nina Bruno Designs again."

"Nina Bruno Designs is the best designer this side of the Mississippi. You'd be a fool not to want to work for us again."

She actually sounded offended.

"Maybe that means I should sleep with *you*," he said.

She shot him one of the looks she'd given Anderson. "I don't rob the cradle."

"Then I guess we have a deal."

She opened her mouth for a retort but, instead, smiled at a large group they skirted a large group

"Not that I'm disappointed," he said, "but where is Tanya, by the way?"

She slowed and her smile wavered. "Over there."

He looked across the sea of bodies in the direction she stared. Tanya stood surrounded by a group of men. The man on her left shifted so that his face came into view and Ben's heart jumped to a hard hammer.

Carlos Sanchez.

The human traffics dealer wasn't supposed to be in Texas.

Chapter 2

Liz stood stock still until Tanya's attention caught on her. The model's gaze flicked to Liz's dress, then her eyes swung back to her face in wide-eyed surprise.

"She seems surprised to see you—or to see you wearing that dress," Adam whispered.

So he'd noticed that, too. Liz, Richard, and Brenda had been so consumed with finding a replacement for Tanya that they automatically concluded she jilted them because Jorge offered her more money. Tanya's reaction, however, suggested something else. She hadn't expected to see the dress at all.

Disbelief turned to fury. Tanya hadn't dumped them for a better offer. She had sabotaged them.

"She decided to play for another team at the last moment, didn't she?" Adam said.

Liz snapped her gaze up to meet his. His attention shifted from the couple to her. She thought she discerned tension in his jaw, but it wasn't there now and he lifted a brow.

"By the look on your face, I'd say I'm right. Who's the competition?" he asked.

Liz hesitated, but realized the news of Tanya's defection was likely scheduled for the next print run of every gossip column in Texas. "Jorge Designs."

"Is that who she's with?"

Liz shifted her attention to Tanya's escort. He was tall, early forties, absolutely gorgeous, with jet black hair and honey brown eyes. The poster boy for the South American gigolo.

"Not Jorge Estonia," she murmured aloud. "And he's too old to be a model."

"So are you."

Liz cut Adam a narrow-eyed glance. "You really know how to sweet talk your boss."

He shrugged. "I'm not the one who said a woman isn't attractive after twenty-five."

"You'll likely think differently when you reach thirty."

He smiled and her heart skipped a beat. His smile could stop traffic. Suddenly, she wondered if she'd been going about selling clothes the wrong way. This man was a dynamite package. His blue eyes smoldered—a stunning combination enhanced by his black tux. Six-foot-four of pure male. No contacts, no drug-induced biceps, just good old-fashioned Mother Nature at her ever-loving best. But despite his looks, it was his smile that truly set him apart from the other models. It didn't matter who wore the dress, only that when a woman wore it, this man would smile at them.

"Why didn't you smile like that for the photo shoot?" Liz asked.

Amusement lit his eyes. "Now that I know you like my smile, I'll be sure to do it more often."

Liz nodded. "You're going to sell my dress for me."

"That's what I'm here for. But you don't give yourself enough credit. You're going to give Tanya a run for her money." He leaned closer and his warm breath brushed her ear as he whispered, "What do you say we go on the offensive and say hello to her and her date?"

Liz imagined Adam's full mouth pressed against her ear. She jarred from the thought. Good Lord, the man was sixteen years her junior—and she was his boss. And he was staring expectantly.

"What?" she blurted.

A very young female model on the arm of a high school graduate slowed as they passed, and Liz realized her outburst had caught their attention. Liz became aware she was squeezing Adam's bicep and started to pull away.

He covered her hand with his. "Nope," he said. "We have to look like we can't live without each other."

Liz glanced down at his hand on hers. The light scratch of calluses against the top of her hand surprised her. Odd. Most male models were as big a prima donna as their female counterparts and seldom lifted a finger for fear a drop of sweat would spoil their looks. But Adam had a down-to-earth quality. Yet tonight, he exuded a dangerous edge that hadn't been present during the photo shoot.

She glanced at Tanya, who had turned her back and was speaking with a group of people. Tanya clutched her date's arm, and Liz knew she was sending a signal: I don't need Nina Bruno Designs.

She would regret that decision.

A waiter passed in front of Liz. Adam released her and snagged two glasses of champagne. He handed one to Liz. She took a large swig. A woman at least sixty years of age raked her gaze down Adam's body. He seemed not to notice and slipped an arm around Liz's waist. Warmth spread through her stomach. Champagne did that to a person. Her second drink nearly emptied the glass.

Liz spotted Larissa Remmey just as the woman turned and met her gaze. The older woman's eyes lit. Attention fixed on Liz, she said something to the man on her right, then started across the room.

Liz smiled and kept her gaze on Larissa as she whispered to Adam, "You get me through this night and there's a bonus in it for you."

"Is it the bonus we discussed earlier?"

"Earlier—" She jerked her gaze onto his face. "I told you, I don't rob the cradle, nor do I mix business with pleasure. Understand?"

"Yes, ma'am," he drawled. "No business with pleasure. I'll be sure to keep them separate."

Liz blinked and wondered whether he had noticed her reaction to him a moment ago. Dammit, she had no one but herself to blame for that. Before she could say more, Larissa reached them and extended her arms.

"Darling," she said with the barest hint of a Russian accent.

Liz shot Adam a quelling look as Larissa pulled her into a cheek hug.

BEN KEPT HIS EXPRESSION CASUAL. HE DIDN'T TYPICALLY LIKE surprises, but Liz Monahan as his date and Texas' most wanted human traffics dealer showing up in El Paso tonight were two surprises he could live with. It looked like he wasn't going to have to go snooping around the Remmey's mansion, after all, to discover their connection to Carlos Sanchez. He could go straight to Sanchez. If he could get the man alone.

Liz slipped her hand through the crook of Ben's arm. Before he could corner Sanchez, he'd have to slip away from

Liz Monahan. He shifted his attention and found himself staring straight down her cleavage. He jerked his gaze up as Larissa said, "So this is the dress we've all been waiting to see." The older woman nodded approval.

Liz laughed, low and sensual, and Ben's groin surprised him by giving a hard salute. He hadn't been this intensely affected when he'd met Laura five years ago. He'd been crazy about her, had even considered marriage. But after two years of dating, he still wasn't home enough to ask her to marry into an empty house, and she simply fell out of love with him.

Staying closer to home won't be a problem with Liz.

The thought brought him up short. He'd thought about her a lot these last two days, but when had he decided he wanted to spend more time at home with a woman? Liz released his arm and Ben resisted the impulse to grasp her hand and put it back. Tonight was about business—for both of them—and he couldn't afford to let her get in his way.

"I doubt you've been waiting all season to see a Nina Bruno design," she said to Larissa.

"On the contrary," Larissa replied. "Your lineup last year was impressive. I've been watching you, as have others. I'm intrigued by the fact you chose to wear the debut dress yourself. Very bold. The leather top fits you to perfection—or I should say, you fill it out to perfection."

Pink tinged Liz's cheeks. "We use the gifts given us," she said.

"And why not?" Larissa said. She turned to Ben. "And who is this luscious thing?"

"Mrs. Remmey, meet Adam Billings," Liz said. "Adam—"

"No introductions are necessary," he cut in. "It's a pleasure to meet you, Mrs. Remmey."

Larissa's eyes lit with pleasure. "Ohh, a charmer." She

stepped closer and curved her fingers around his arm. "I think you'll be my pet for the evening."

"Pet for the evening?" a female voice said.

Even as Ben registered the familiar voice, the speaker stepped into view. He froze. The last person he expected to see was Assistant DA Sheila Antonio. He couldn't allow her to discover that Carlos Sanchez occupied the same room with her.

Ben snapped from a brain freeze and said, "You're Sheila Antonio." He extended a hand. "Adam Billings. I'm a big fan."

Her brows lifted in an expression of polite curiosity. She slid her hand into his and gave a hard squeeze, intended to remind him of their last encounter.

He felt the curious gazes of Liz and Mrs. Remmey and flashed his most charming grin. "You made big news last year when you prosecuted that drug dealer the Border Patrol caught with two kilos of cocaine. The guy put out a hit on you, but that didn't stop you from putting him away for twenty years."

"Not Border Patrol," Sheila said. "The Texas Rangers caught him."

"What's the difference?"

"There's a world of difference." A glint appeared in her eyes. "They didn't catch the man contracted to kill me."

They weren't supposed to. He was the hitman, and she knew it.

"Isn't he delicious?" Mrs. Remmey interjected.

Sheila nodded. "Yes, he is."

"But he's spoken for." Mrs. Remmey glanced at Liz. "You don't mind, do you, darling?"

"My escort is your escort," Liz replied.

Ben glanced at Sanchez. The man laughed at something

another guest said. Ben had to break free of the women. He couldn't chance Sanchez leaving the party.

"We'll talk later, Sheila," Mrs. Remmey said. "I have to show off Liz to my other guests."

"It was very nice to meet you, Ms. Antonio," Ben said.

She inclined her head. "Perhaps we'll have a chance to talk more later?"

"I wouldn't count on it," Mrs. Remmey said. "I plan to keep him to myself." She started away and Ben turned his attention to her. "Come along, Liz," she said. "I believe tonight is going to be your lucky night."

Chapter 3

Liz's excitement grew as Larissa Remmey worked the room. Two small but respectable boutiques fawned over the dress—after Larissa informed them the dress was sure to be a hit. They begged appointments early next week and Liz promised her assistant would call them first thing Monday morning.

Larissa then left with Adam to, as she said, "show off my newest friend" and make all the other women at the party jealous. Liz released a silent breath and accepted a glass of champagne from the tray of a passing waiter as she milled about the room. The evening's rocky start might just end in financial salvation. No thanks to Tanya.

Liz scanned the room until she spotted Tanya on the dancefloor. She sipped her champagne and stared until Tanya's eyes met hers. Their gazes locked no more than a second before Tanya's date whirled her, but the anxiety in Tanya's eyes said she had gotten the message Liz telepathed: I know you sabotaged us.

Liz jarred from her thoughts when Adam came into view, dancing with Sheila Antonio. Liz recognized Sheila's interest in him. In her job, Liz watched women fawn over male models, but Sheila Antonio's attitude bordered on proprietary. Lust came in all forms and, in this case, the form was five foot eight with blonde hair coiled atop her head, and an hourglass figure that would make any full-bodied model jealous.

She'd draped an arm around Adam's neck like a familiar lover and now stared at him as if intending to eat him on the spot. Adam stared politely down at her, though Liz was certain she detected frustration in his expression. Sheila's hand slid from Adam's neck and she flattened her palm against his chest. He maneuvered a turn and Liz realized he would see her gawking. She whirled away and snatched a shrimp appetizer from the tray of a passing waiter.

"Ms. Monahan."

The male voice startled Liz and she turned to face the speaker.

The tall, dark-haired man flashed a smile. "I'm Reid Lowman." He extended a hand.

Liz shook his hand and didn't miss the flick of his eyes to her chest. If buyers noticed his attention, they would buy the dress and promise to make their customers the belle of the ball in this latest Nina Bruno design.

"I had no idea Nina Bruno's Creative Director would be modeling this year's winter debut design," he said.

That made two of them. "Life is full of surprises." She tried to pull her hand free. He held fast. "Who are you representing tonight?" she asked.

"Larissa invited me—which means I'm free for the evening."

"Ms. Monahan has a date for the evening."

Liz turned at the sound of Adam's voice, and Reid released her hand as Adam slipped an arm around her waist.

Reid gave Adam an assessing look and a corner of his mouth lifted. He returned his attention to her, reached inside his front jacket pocket, and handed her a card. "Give me a call when you drop off the help this evening. I'm a night owl."

She took the card. "I'll put you in my contacts for future reference."

His smile suggested a personal contact instead of a professional one.

He left and Adam's hand shifted to her spine as he urged her in the opposite direction. "Is sex really how you sell designs?" he asked.

Liz shifted her gaze to his face. "Why do you think women wear designer clothes?"

"Because the fashion industry convinces women they have to pimp themselves out."

"You're very naive, Mr. Billings. Women have been pimping themselves out since the first male showed interest in a female."

Something undefined flickered in his eyes and was replaced by grudging respect. "That dress'll get the job done," he said. "But do you really need that guy?"

She laughed. "He's just another model trying to get a leg up."

"Trying to get your leg up," Adam said. "I suppose that's a requirement for getting the job?"

Liz's amusement died. "That's not how I hired you, if you recall."

"True. But maybe you didn't like me."

"I like your *looks* just fine."

He grinned. "Ms. Monahan, I do believe I've made you angry."

It was her turn to be surprised. He had pushed her buttons—twice in fact—a feat not easily accomplished.

Which meant she was the one who hadn't separated business from pleasure. Liz spotted a dress she was sure had been copied from another designer's previous winter collection. That eliminated them from the competition.

"How did you manage to escape—" she started to say 'Ms. Antonio,' realized he'd know she'd been watching them dance, and managed, instead, "—Larissa?"

"I told her I had to save you from the wolves."

Liz riveted her gaze onto him. "Wolves?" Her outburst earned her a curious look from a man to her left. She urged Adam two paces away, then whispered, "That's not your job description. You're supposed to make me look good."

"Then I'd better get to it."

He grasped her hand and she startled at the gentle pressure or his fingers on hers as he worked his way through the crowd. They neared the orchestra and she registered the waltz they played—and Adam's intentions.

"Mr. Billings," she began, but he turned and slipped a hand around her waist.

Adam drew her into a tight turn and her pulse quickened as her breasts flattened against his chest. She glanced down and couldn't halt a small gasp at seeing her breasts straining against her bodice. Liz looked up to find him staring down at her, one brow raised.

She narrowed her eyes. "You're going to get us arrested."

He gave a low chuckle that carried with it something indefinable. "There's a first time for everything."

The firm pressure of his fingers on her back tightened as he deftly steered her away from a couple dancing too close. "You're enjoying this," she said under her breath.

Another laugh.

What was up with this man? She had seen a lot of shameless flirting and blunt propositioning in her years in the fashion industry—not to mention, the three years as Creative Director for Nina Bruno Designs—but she had never been... What? Accosted? Worse, she had to admit, was the fact that it had been some time since a man held her so intimately. Adam sidestepped another couple, executing an expert turn. Liz's grip on his back tightened and her fingers brushed the soft hair at his neck. A shiver raced down her spine. She grimaced inwardly. It really had been too long since she'd done anything except access men for their ability to make a model look good.

The song ended and relief kicked in. A slower song began and Liz hurried to pull away, but his hold tightened.

"We haven't gotten everyone's attention yet." He pulled her closer and slipped his leg between hers.

Her head swam when the steely thigh muscles pressed her leg as he swayed with the music.

Eyes locked with hers, he placed her hand against his chest. "Relax, Ms. Monahan, you're the gem of the ball. You're supposed to be enjoying the party."

"I'm supposed to be working."

"That means playing the part of a woman who's full of life, who knows she's adored. Isn't that what Tanya would be doing if she was wearing that dress?"

He had a point, damn him, but she answered, "As you pointed out, I'm no model."

He leaned close and pressed his jaw to her cheek. "You say that like it's a bad thing." His voice, low and deep, sent another shiver down her back. "You're a real woman," he said. "Not one of those made-up paper dolls."

His thigh brushed the juncture between her legs. Liz became aware of the warmth of his hand on her back. She held her breath, half expecting his fingers to slide down over the curve of her buttocks. But his gentle pressure remained confident and warm on the small of her back.

"Those made-up paper dolls sell dresses," she managed in a voice that came out low and breathy.

"Trust me, you're the best advertisement Nina Bruno could have gotten for this dress."

"I won't be propositioned, Mr. Billings." She closed her eyes and gave thanks that her voice held more conviction than she felt.

"When I proposition you, Ms. Monahan, you'll know it."

"I'm old enough to be your mother," she said. "And don't say *but you're not my mother*. I *am* your boss."

"Two points we'll discuss later," he said.

She snapped her head up. He smiled and her stomach flipped. Had she lost her mind? She dealt with gorgeous men every day. Why did this one evoke such giddy flutters?

The smile. That's what did her in. *That smile will sell dresses*, she admonished herself. *Remember that and nothing else.*

"Right now we have more pressing issues." he said.

"Excuse me?"

Liz bumped into a hard body behind her. She whirled and something hard struck her hip. Adam turned with her, not missing a sway to the musical beat. She'd bumped into Tanya's date.

"Forgive me," Tanya's date's cultured Mexican accent caught Liz's attention. He made eye contact while still dancing with Tanya. "I hope I did not hurt you."

Liz smiled. "Not at all." Was that a gun she'd struck?

"My fault completely," Adam interjected. "I was distracted."

The man's eyes remained fixed on Liz. "I see why."

From the corner of her eye, she saw Tanya purse her lips.

"Nice to see you, Tanya," Adam said.

Tanya flashed a bored smile. "I don't recall your name."

"Adam," Liz cut in, "you were just about to get me some champagne. If you will excuse us." She nodded at the couple, then pulled free of Adam and led him from the dance floor."

"What was that all about?" she demanded once they were several paces from the nearest guests.

His gaze returned to the couple. "What do you mean?"

"You intended to confront her."

Adam looked at her, brow furrowed. "All I did was say hello."

"You purposely bumped into them."

"I'm an excellent dancer. He bumped into us."

"You said you were distracted," she hissed.

He shrugged. "I was being polite. I didn't peg you as being so easily intimidated."

"I'm not. But I have some sense."

Liz caught sight of Larissa. The older woman's eyes shifted to Adam's face. She smiled and crooked a finger in a *come here* motion.

"Seems your benefactor is requesting our presence," he said.

"*Your* presence," Liz corrected.

"We'll work that to our advantage."

He grasped her hand and started toward Larissa.

He held her hand lightly, but firmly. If she tugged free it would be obvious she wasn't pleased. "I promised a bonus if you got me through the night," she said under her breath. "Make a scene with Tanya, and I'll bury you."

His head snapped in her direction. Finally, she'd gotten his attention.

"I believe you mean it," he said.

She couldn't tell if he was worried or amused. "Don't try me," she said.

"I think it would be worth seeing you try," he replied.

"What the—I'll do more than try—"

She broke off as Larissa stepped away from the woman she'd been talking with and took three steps to meet them.

"Darlings," she cooed, "I want to introduce you to a dear friend of mine. Martin," Larissa called to a man standing a few feet away. "Come here, darling."

Liz turned her attention to the short, wiry man who joined their group.

He reached Larissa's side and said in a British accent, "The party is marvelous, Larissa. And you look smashing." He kissed her cheek. "Where is that granddaughter of yours? You promised she would be here. I brought her something special from London."

"Christina is under the weather," Larissa replied.

"Poor thing," Martin said. "Nothing serious, I hope."

"Just a cold, but I insisted she rest."

"Of course. I'll have the gift sent round tomorrow. It's an outfit designed by Chelsea that will look smashing on her. Don't worry," he quickly added, "it's appropriate for a fifteen-year-old."

Larissa laughed, but Liz thought she sounded tired.

"I trust you completely," Larissa said. "And I'm sure she'll love it. Now, I want to introduce you to the designer I was telling you about last month. Liz Monahan with Nina Bruno Designs. Liz, meet Martin Stayes, head buyer for LaRouche."

For a heartbeat, Liz couldn't think.

Martin Stayes...LaRouche?

LaRouche—one of the most exclusive boutiques in London? She resisted an impulse to leap and shout *yes!* and barely managed a casual, "Very nice to meet you, Mr. Stayes."

"Well, any designer friend of Larissa's is a designer friend of mine," he said.

"And, Martin, darling," Larissa said, "in case you didn't know it, Liz is wearing Nina Bruno's newest confection."

"The dress you told me about?" he asked.

"The one and only."

He turned his attention to Liz and ran his gaze down her body. "The dress is stunning, and she fills it out beautifully."

"Of course she does." Larissa winked at Liz. "Now, I'm sure you two have business to discuss and, as we all know, Liz never mixes business with pleasure. I, on the other hand, have no such compunctions. So I'm stealing this young man from you again, Liz dear. I think, this time, I'll keep him."

Chapter 4

"Very nice of you to introduce Ms. Monahan to your friend," Ben said once he and Larissa were out of earshot.

Her lips twitched in amusement. "Do you know who he is?"

"No. But I'm betting you wouldn't waste your time introducing her to a nobody."

"I don't know any nobodies," she said.

Ben laughed. "I'm sure you don't. Did you see Tanya?"

"Oh, yes. She's with Carlos Sanchez."

"I don't believe I know him, either."

Larissa slanted him a curious glance. "I don't believe I know *you*, darling."

Ben flashed a smile, one he knew had stopped more than one woman in her tracks. "I'm just one more working model."

"I know every *working* model in this town. You're not on that list."

"Can you keep a secret?" he asked.

"I'm the soul of discretion."

"I'm working on my masters in biotechnology at the

University of Texas." He shrugged. "Education is expensive. A friend suggested I do a bit of modeling to make ends meet."

Her brows rose. "Biotechnology?"

"Are you saying a man can't have looks and brains?" he asked.

"On the contrary, I suspect you have a great many brains."

"You're a terrible flirt, Mrs. Remmey."

"Don't worry," she said. "My husband isn't the jealous type."

"Lucky me," Ben said.

"Indeed," she replied. "So, shall we find out why Tanya is here with Carlos Sanchez and wearing Jorge Estonia's dress instead of that delicious confection Liz is wearing?"

Ben smiled. "You are a troublemaker, Mrs. Remmey."

She squeezed his bicep. "Then I am in good company."

THE PROBLEM, BEN REALIZED TWENTY MINUTES LATER AS LARISSA hugged yet another model, was escorting a woman everyone liked. He didn't blame them, but even two minutes was enough time for Sanchez to slip through the door. Ben had considered excusing himself from Larissa and simply walking up to Sanchez and talking with him. In the end, though, what he had to say demanded privacy. If Sanchez gave him any trouble, being in a crowded room could get Ben killed.

Larissa murmured something to the young model then faced Ben. "I'm sorry, darling. I know you're anxious to be done with this business."

Ben flashed a smile. "There's no business more pressing than you, Mrs. Remmey."

She slipped her hand into the crook of his arm. "Larissa, and, please, we can be honest with one another. Wouldn't you agree?" She drew him away at a sedate stroll.

"Of course," he said.

"They make an interesting couple, don't they?"

"Who?"

A corner of her mouth lifted. "Honesty, remember?"

Ben knew better than to hesitate. "All right, Larissa, why don't you tell me what you have in mind?"

She looked at him, her smile wide. "The direct approach. I like that. I have in mind us solving one another's problems."

Ben lifted a brow in question.

"I will take care of her." Larissa angled her head discreetly to the right. He didn't have to look to know she meant Tanya. Larissa smiled as if they were sharing an intimate moment. "If you take care of him."

Ben's mind snapped to full attention, but he managed in a casual tone, "Take *care* of him?"

"You know I am Russian, yes?"

"Yes, ma'am. The slight accent gives you away."

Her voice softened. "When I came here, I was a sensation. I was very beautiful, which is why Francis married me."

"You are still very beautiful."

She laughed. "I was right. You are a charmer. Well, what you do not know—I think—is that my father was Russian mafia."

"No," Ben admitted, "I didn't know that."

"It was long ago," she said. "But you never forget such a life." Ben was startled to detect pain in her words. "One lasting effect," she went on, "is that I still recognize one of their kind quite easily."

His step nearly faltered and a hot rush charged up his spine, the kind felt when one steps on a nail. It doesn't hurt so much at first, but the shock and anticipation of yanking that nail out turned the stomach.

"Mrs. Remmey—"

She looked at him. "I love my husband, young man."

Ben paused. "I'm sure you do, ma'am."

She wrinkled her nose. "That makes me sound so old."

Ben blinked, then couldn't help a smile. "Forgive me, Larissa."

She beamed. "Now, then. I will take care of her. You take care of him."

Ben kept his voice neutral. "What do you suggest I do?"

"I will arrange privacy. But first, we must do something with that pistol strapped to your ankle."

This time he blurted, "I beg your pardon?"

"Young man, I can just as easily recognize an officer of the law as I can a member of the mob."

They reached a private corner of the room and Ben stopped cold. He glanced around. The nearest guests conversed fifteen feet away. He shifted his attention back to Larissa. "You're very observant, Mrs. Remmey."

"As I said, one never forgets."

He nodded. "Have you confided this information to anyone else?"

"My husband."

"What is his connection to Mr. Sanchez?" Ben asked. This he had to know.

She released a tired sigh. "Carlos has something very important that belongs to us."

"What is that?"

"Our granddaughter."

"The sick granddaughter?" he demanded.

She gave an almost imperceptible nod and moisture appeared in her eyes. "Our son and his wife died in a car accident when she was four. We have raised her this last eleven years. She is the world to us."

A Mack truck of memory struck and propelled Ben a

month into the past to the day he found two dead girls on the El Paso/Juarez border. His heart thudded. He headed the Ranger Reconnaissance Team that had tracked their kidnappers into the desert. The blood that had pooled beneath the young women on the hard ground had turned thick and sticky inside of two hours. Now, the man ultimately responsible for their deaths stood twenty feet away chatting with some of El Paso's most upstanding and influential citizens.

Fury fermented into rage and Ben saw himself walking up to Sanchez and arresting him. The twenty-two strapped to Ben's ankle would keep the human traffics dealer in check—despite the gun Sanchez hid beneath his coat. Ben stuffed a hand into his trousers pocket and unclenched the fist he hadn't realized he'd made.

He couldn't arrest Sanchez without the half dozen South American bodyguards who roamed the ballroom slaughtering every guest in the room in order to save their boss. And arresting Sanchez wouldn't save the Remmey's granddaughter. Ben had to stop her from becoming another of the thousands of girls who ended up in a rich sheik's harem or as a rich businessman's sex slave—or worse, a prostitute in one of the brothels that served hundreds of men daily.

"Is there someplace we can go where you can fill me in?" Ben asked Larissa.

"Smile, darling," she said.

For an instant Ben wasn't sure what she'd said, then the rough edge that had leeched into his voice registered. Dammit. He had to maintain control.

"Mr. Sanchez is watching us," she whispered.

Ben flashed a smile and leaned close as if in intimate conversation. "Why would he be watching us?"

"Because my husband is talking to him about a meeting with you."

Anticipation ramped up like a live electrical wire. "I suppose you'd better give me the rundown now, then." Something occurred to Ben. "Why is Sanchez escorting Tanya?"

"That came as a surprise to me," Larissa replied.

Ben didn't like that. "All right. What does Sanchez want from you?"

"He wants my husband to smuggle women across the border when he buys textiles."

Suddenly the missing pieces all clicked into place.

When the FBI showed up on the Rangers' doorstep three days ago, they demanded information on Sanchez's contacts in Texas. Millionaire Francis Remmey had just appeared on the Rangers' radar. No one knew why an upstanding citizen was suddenly in bed with a human traffics dealer. The Feds planned a sting operation intended to uncover the connection, but the whole thing came to a screeching halt twelve hours later.

The high-brow world of fashion didn't welcome outsiders. They needed someone who would be accepted at a moment's notice—and they needed that someone fast. Ben's good looks put him at the top of the list. The pressure the governor applied to the Feds to catch the girls' killers forced them to partner with the Rangers.

In the space of an hour, Ben had Sanchez in his sights and discovered the connection between the slaver and Remmey. The FBI would take Sanchez into custody once the Rangers arrested him. But first, the Rangers could extract some important information in the process. And that's exactly what Ben planned on doing *tonight*.

"I'LL BE BACK IN LONDON NEXT MONDAY," MARTIN TOLD LIZ. "Have your assistant call me to set up a conference."

"I'll do that," Liz replied.

"I will let Brenda know to expect your call," he said.

Liz's excitement soared, but she forced a casual smile and murmured, "Thank you, Mr. Stayes."

He shook his head. "No thanks necessary. Nina Bruno is a small firm, but I'm sure there isn't a model here who doesn't know who you are."

She was surprised by the sudden change in topic, but gave a deferential cant of her head. "I've worked with a fair number of models."

"I'm sure you have," he said, "but the looks they're giving you have nothing to do with wanting jobs. And they're not the only ones who have noticed you."

Liz glimpsed a mature man with a beautiful young woman on his arm glance at her chest. Thank God Richard wasn't here to witness their victory. He would likely insist that she wear the damn dress to every scheduled event through the remainder of the season. *LaRouche* was the break Nina Bruno Designs needed. One exclusive international buyer had the potential to skyrocket them to success—and bail them out of the crippling debt they now faced.

She grabbed a glass of champagne from a passing waiter and smiled at Martin. "You're very kind."

"If the rest of your winter line is half as provocative as that dress, we'll be doing a lot of business," he said.

As Liz sipped the champagne, her attention caught on Adam. He stood in a corner, his ear bent toward Larissa Remmey's mouth. Larissa was clearly enjoying his company, and he was doing his job by making her feel like the only woman in the world. If Larissa was happy, she would tell everyone that she had discovered Nina Bruno's jewel of a debut design. Tonight had exceeded expectations.

"If I was you, I would smile, darling," Martin said.

Liz shifted her gaze to follow his stare and her heartrate kicked up at sight of the woman looking at them. Michelle Alvarez, *the* top fashion reporter in the country. Beside her, Jason Wells, the only photographer Michelle ever used, held his camera pointed at them. Liz smiled in time for the flash.

"Your dress will likely appear on every fashion blog and twitter feed," Martin said. "With you wearing it."

Liz snapped her gaze onto him. Amusement sparkled in his eyes.

"You have a mean streak, Mr. Stayes."

"You aren't the first to point that out. If you'll excuse me, I believe I see someone I know." He started away, then paused and said, "Call me Martin when you phone next week."

Before she could reply, he walked away. Liz took a swig of champagne. She would likely need another glass.

Sheila Antonio step up beside her. "He's absolutely scrumptious, isn't he?" Sheila said.

Liz didn't have to look in the direction Sheila stared to know she referred to Adam Billings. "He was the perfect choice for the job," Liz said.

"You and he aren't...friends?" Sheila asked.

"I met him at the job interview."

"I don't know how you can resist in this case."

She couldn't forget the seventeen-year age—difference despite his stunning looks. "You learn," Liz said.

Sheila returned her attention to her. "He's a free agent, then?"

"He will be after tonight." Liz smiled. "This is a paid assignment. Our contract specifies the models are not to mix work with pleasure."

The younger woman angled her head. "I fully understand. Might I ask how you came to hire...Adam, was his name?"

Liz kept her expression neutral. It never ceased to amaze her how women would practically fall into bed with a young, gorgeous model without knowing more than his name. In this case, the woman wasn't even sure of that.

"He came to us through one of the agencies we use."

"I've never seen him before," Sheila said. "I would remember a face like that."

And the body and—the smile. That smile. "He's modeled in Paris and London," she said. "This is his first big job in the States."

"I see." Sheila took a glass of champagne from a passing waiter. "I understand you aren't a professional model. You're Head of Creative Designs for Nina Bruno. Isn't it unusual for an executive to model? Aren't you taking a risk?"

Liz wanted to thump the woman upside the head. Leave it to a lawyer to ask all the right—or wrong—questions. "Our model had a last minute conflict." She resisted the urge to dart a glance at Tanya, who was surrounded by several older men. Without a doubt, Ms. Sheila D.A. Antonio would notice.

"What brings you to the gala?" Liz asked, and instantly regretted the question. Young, male models could be what brought her to the gala.

"I met Larissa a year ago. We share a mutual friend, Senator Ross Pierson."

"Roos the Boos Pierson?" Liz asked.

Sheila nodded. "You know him?"

"I do. He went to law school with my father. I didn't realize he had a home here in El Paso. How do you know him?"

"One of the partners of the law firm I worked for in

Houston is friends with the senator. I saw him at parties. We became fast friends. He's a straight shooter."

"He is," Liz agreed, and grudgingly admitted that Sheila Antonio had some strong, good qualities to be close friends with Senator Pierson. Of course, there was always the chance Sheila overstated their friendship. She wouldn't be the first woman to cozy up to Roos the Boos Pierson. At sixty, he was still an attractive man.

Sheila reached into her clutch bag and pulled out a card and a pen. She set her drink on a nearby table, then jotted down a phone number and handed the card to Liz. "The senator has a party planned tomorrow for some of the local pro football players. I'm betting he would love to see you."

"I'm returning to Dallas tomorrow," Liz said. "But I'll give him a call. It's been too long since I've spoken with him. Thank you, Ms. Antonio."

"Call me Sheila. We're practically old friends ourselves."

There it was. Sheila's version of friendship.

Liz laughed. "Sheila. Thanks."

"Thank you," Sheila said.

"For what?"

"For bringing *him* to the party."

Liz looked in the direction Sheila nodded and watched Larissa slide her hand into the crook of Adam's arm. They entered the crowd, headed toward the foyer.

"It looks like Larissa knows a good thing when she sees it," Sheila said.

Shock froze Liz's gaze on the doorway Larissa and Adam had stepped through. Surely, Adam Billings wouldn't fraternize with the woman hosting the fashion event of the season?

* 9 7 8 1 0 8 8 2 5 8 5 6 9 *